PEN PALS:
BOOK THIRTE

LISA,
WE MISS YOU

by Sharon Dennis Wyeth

A YEARLING BOOK

Published by
Dell Publishing
a division of
Bantam Doubleday Dell Publishing Group, Inc.
666 Fifth Avenue
New York, New York 10103

ISBN: 0-440-40393-6

Illustrations by Wendy Wax
Published by arrangement with Parachute Press, Inc.
Printed in the United States of America
September 1990
10 9 8 7 6 5 4 3 2 1
OPM

Dear Readers,

This book is dedicated to you. Thanks for your letters!

Happy reading always,
Sharon Dennis Wyeth

CHAPTER 1

———◆———

Dear Shanon,
I can't wait until the first day of school when I can see you again! I really miss you. When we get back to Alma Stephens, let's you and I be the very first to walk Maggie and Dan's new puppy!

Love,
Lisa

P.S. Rob is still my pen pal. Have you been writing to Mars? See you soon in Fox Hall, Suite 3-D, with Amy and Palmer! Foxes of the Third Dimension, FOREVER!

The last days of summer had sped by like lightning, and now thirteen-year-old Shanon Davis was on her way back to boarding school. She could hardly wait to see her pretty dark-haired roommate, Lisa McGreevy, and the two other girls who shared their suite—Palmer Durand and Amy Ho. Though Shanon's family lived in the nearby town of Brighton, she hadn't stepped foot on the Alma Stephens campus since the beginning of summer. The all-girls' school had been practically deserted by everyone except the headmistress, Miss Pryn, and a few of the older faculty. But now, as her parents' station wagon turned into the winding driveway that led to Fox Hall, Shanon saw a blur of familiar faces: Gina Hawkins, Muffin Talbot, Kate Majors. . . .

Shanon waved out of the window. It was great to see everyone! But the people she really wanted to see were Lisa, Amy, and Palmer.

Her freshman year at Alma Stephens had been the most amazing time in Shanon's life, thanks in large part to her suitemates—Lisa especially. Shanon's outgoing roommate was always full of ideas. She was the one who had convinced all of them to write to boy pen pals. And after living together for nine months, Shanon thought of Lisa as her very best friend. . . .

"Stop!" Shanon cried, leaning forward. "Double-park in front of the dorm, Dad! Here come Amy and Palmer!"

Mr. Davis had barely stopped the station wagon before Shanon bounded from the backseat and dashed toward the dormitory. Amy Ho and Palmer Durand were already running to meet her.

"Shanon!" cried Amy.

"Amy! Palmer!"

The three girls hugged and started talking all at once.

"You look great!" Palmer said to Shanon.

"Thanks," Shanon replied. "So do you! You look great too, Amy!"

They stood back, admiring each other's outfits. Palmer Durand was wearing a silk dress in turquoise blue, her favorite color. Her wavy blond hair was held back with a matching bow. Dark-haired Amy Ho, who almost always dressed in black, was wearing a bright red jumper with a crisp white blouse underneath. "A back-to-school present from my mom," she said, rolling her eyes. Shanon's new cotton dress was pale green.

"Your hair got long again," Amy told Shanon.

"It looks a lot lighter, too," said Palmer.

Shanon giggled. "You mean it's not mousey brown any-more?"

"It looks almost golden," Palmer insisted. "Must be from the sun. It's gorgeous!"

"Thanks," said Shanon, flushing with pleasure. "Where's Lisa? I can't wait to see her."

"She's not here yet," said Amy.

"Coming through!" Mr. Davis appeared at the foot of the stairs with Shanon's trunk. Mrs. Davis stood behind, holding a suitcase. Shanon, Amy, and Palmer quickly parted, creating a path for them.

"Hi, Mr. and Mrs. Davis," Amy said.

"Hi there, girls," said Shanon's mother. "Did you all have a nice summer?"

"It was okay," Palmer replied unenthusiastically. "That is, if you like California."

"You girls in the same place as last year?" Mr. Davis called over his shoulder.

"Suite 3-D!" Amy volunteered.

"Best suite in Fox Hall," Shanon declared with a smile. "I'm so glad things are the same as last year."

Mr. and Mrs. Davis disappeared into the dorm. With Amy and Palmer beside her, Shanon returned to the car for the rest of her luggage.

"So what's this about California?" Shanon asked Palmer. "I thought you were spending the summer with your mother in Florida."

3

Palmer shrugged. "The last part of August I visited my dad in L.A. Actually, it would have been fun if Georgette hadn't been there."

"Palmer's sister is going to be at Alma this year," said Amy.

"Stepsister," Palmer corrected her. "She's my dad's wife's daughter."

"Still . . ." said Shanon, "that's great! Having somebody in your family at school should be fun."

"You don't know Georgette," Palmer protested.

Shanon and Amy dragged a big duffel bag out of the station wagon, while Palmer grabbed an overnight case from the front seat. As the three girls headed into Fox Hall, they almost collided with Shanon's parents, who were on their way out.

"So long, Pumpkin," Mrs. Davis said, giving Shanon a kiss on the cheek.

Shanon put down her end of the duffel bag. "See you, Mom," she said with a hug.

"Don't forget you're coming home in a few weekends for Nana's seventieth birthday," Shanon's dad said, putting an arm on her shoulder.

"I won't forget," Shanon promised.

"Maybe you two girls might like to come, too," Mrs. Davis said on her way to the car.

"And Lisa, of course!" Mr. Davis put in. "Tell her 'Hi' for us!"

"I will, Dad," Shanon replied, smiling. "Bye, Mom! I'll call you next weekend!"

Amy and Shanon picked up the duffel bag again. Still carrying the overnight case, Palmer led the way into Fox

4

Hall. In the front corridor they bumped into their young faculty resident.

"Welcome back!" the teacher said.

"Hi, Miss Grayson!" Shanon said brightly.

"It's Ms. Grayson-Griffith, now that she's married," Amy whispered as they climbed up the stairs.

"See you later, Ms. Grayson-Griffith," Shanon giggled. "Can I drop by a little later? I want to see Gracie!"

"Cutest dog in New Hampshire," Maggie Grayson-Griffith called after them. "Still an ankle-biter, however," she added, laughing. "Come by as soon as you're settled!"

Still giggling, the girls reached the third floor and Suite 3-D. Amy pushed open the door with her foot, and she and Shanon dropped the big bag they'd been carrying.

"I don't know what you've got in there," Amy teased, "but I think it's been good for my biceps."

"It *is* kind of heavy," Shanon agreed. "My dad made me wooden bookends, and I stuck them in with the new bedspreads my mom made for me and Lisa. I've got some books in there, too, and also a few presents."

"Presents?" Palmer exclaimed with a greedy gleam in her big blue eyes.

"Hold your horses," Shanon said. "Let's wait for Lisa." She looked around the cozy sitting room and sighed with pleasure. "Our suite really is the best one in the dorm!"

"Looks like the same old dump to me," Palmer groused, stepping over the duffel bag, "except they slapped a new coat of paint on."

"I didn't even notice," Shanon said in surprise.

"That's because it's the same color as last year," said Amy, crossing into her bedroom.

5

"Not quite," Shanon decided, examining the walls. "This shade is just a *little* lighter." She wrinkled her nose. "I liked it better the old way—it was pinker."

"Putrid peach." Palmer turned up her nose. "And that pink loveseat," she added, shaking her head in dismay.

"I love the loveseat!" Shanon protested. She dragged her bag across the sitting room. "I love everything in our suite." Pausing at her bedroom door, she saw that everything was just the same as last year: the familiar twin beds, the desk and chairs, the big dresser. The only thing missing was the sunflower poster that Lisa had taken home for the summer.

"Come and see what my mom made!" Shanon sang out. Hoisting her bag onto a chair, she unzipped it, pulled out two flowered spreads, and dumped one on each bed.

Amy bounced into the room. "Nice," she said, fingering the soft cotton fabric.

"Where are the presents?" Palmer asked, joining them.

Shanon giggled. "Okay, I'll give them to you now. I guess Lisa won't mind." Fishing around in the bag, she came up with two identical canvas-covered books.

"Notebooks?" Palmer said with a frown.

"Journals," Shanon replied, presenting one to each of the girls.

"As in diaries?" Palmer asked. "That's different! I love diaries."

"Me, too," said Amy. "It's nice to have something to jot things down in. Thanks."

"I got the same exact kind for me and Lisa, too," Shanon explained as she started to unpack. "I already wrote some stuff in mine."

6

"About Mars, I bet!" Palmer teased.

Shanon blushed. "As a matter of fact, Mars has been on my mind a lot. This summer he wrote me the neatest—"

As the front door to the suite clicked opened, Shanon let out a gasp. "It's Lisa!" She bolted out into the front room, then stopped abruptly. It wasn't Lisa who had come in at all, but a short, pretty blonde.

"Hi," the girl said. "I'm Georgette Durand."

"Hi," Shanon said back. "I'm Shanon Davis."

Palmer walked up to the younger girl. "I told you I would come to *your* room," she greeted her coldly.

"When's that going to be?" the pretty girl asked.

Palmer sighed, her impatience showing. "When I get finished here!"

"I just thought I'd remind you," Georgette pouted. "Even Dad says your memory isn't the greatest."

Palmer's blue eyes flashed. "Dad said that? When?"

"When we were on the way to the airport and you forgot your suitcase," Georgette countered.

"Forgetting a suitcase isn't the same thing as forgetting a person," Palmer said shortly. And with that, she led Georgette to the door. "I'll see you later."

"Wow," Amy breathed the minute Georgette was gone. "You really gave your kid sister a hard time."

"*Step*sister," said Palmer.

Amy shrugged. "You may not be real sisters, but you still look alike."

"There may be some slight resemblance when it comes to our looks," Palmer said hotly, "but when it comes to our personalities there's absolutely nothing that's similar! Georgette is a total pain. She drives me crazy."

7

"Let's go back into my room," Shanon suggested to change the subject. "There's something I want to show you."

"Our pen pal picture!" Amy exclaimed as Shanon pulled a framed photograph out of her suitcase. "It's the one we had taken last year with John, Rob, Sam, and Mars."

"Only this is an enlargement!" Palmer exclaimed.

"Eight by ten," Shanon said with pride. "I took the negative home and had it blown up. Let's keep it in the sitting room, just like last year."

"Good thinking," said Amy, admiring the photograph. "That way we can all look at it."

"I could stare at it all day," Palmer sighed. "I think that's the best picture of Sam I've ever seen. I love the way he has his arm around me."

"You and Sam are very photogenic," Amy agreed.

"I think it's a good picture of Lisa, too," said Shanon. "I love those earrings she's wearing." She wandered to the window. "Speaking of Lisa, I wonder where she is."

"Probably dropping her brother, Reggie, at Ardsley Academy," Amy said just as the front door clicked open again.

"There she is!" cried Shanon.

The three girls dashed into the front room. But instead of Lisa, they found a man in a gray chauffeur's uniform.

"Suite 3-D?" the stranger asked.

"This is it," said Amy, glancing at him quizzically.

Turning on his heel, the man disappeared for a moment and then returned with a big trunk.

"Gee," Palmer said, nudging Shanon, "Lisa's folks must have hired a driver."

"I guess so," said Shanon. "If that's Lisa McGreevy's

8

trunk, you can put it in there," she said, pointing to her bedroom.

"I don't know any Miss McGravy," the chauffeur replied, leaving the trunk by the door.

"*McGreevy*—not *McGravy*," said Amy.

"I beg your pardon," the chauffeur said before walking out again. "But that trunk is the property of Max Schloss."

"Max who?" called Amy. The chauffeur didn't turn back.

"*Schloss*," Palmer said, reading the tag on the trunk. "Max Schloss."

"Who in the world is that?" asked Shanon. "And what is his trunk doing in our room?"

"Maybe Alma's gone coeducational," Amy piped up hopefully.

"I think we'd have heard about it before now," Shanon said. She examined the oversized trunk curiously. "This thing must weigh a ton. I hope that chauffeur's going to come back to move it."

"He will when he finds out he has the wrong suite," Palmer assured her.

"Max Schloss," mused Amy. "What a strange-sounding name. I have a feeling I've heard it before."

"It's totally weird," chuckled Palmer. "Sounds like someone's grandfather."

"Of course," said Shanon. "Some girl in Fox Hall probably borrowed her grandfather's trunk and forgot to take the tag off. I don't think it's Lisa's," she added. "Her grandparents' last name is definitely not Schloss."

"Schloss, floss," joked Palmer. "Maybe his real name's Max Dental Floss."

9

Amy let out a shrill giggle. "Some old guy with a tooth problem. I just hope he—"

She broke off in mid-sentence as a tall, red-haired girl in a dark-green, fringed leather jacket stepped through the doorway. She was carrying an armful of dresses on padded silk hangers. "Be careful bringing up the CD player, Ollie," she called over her shoulder. "And don't forget my trombone!" Marching into the room, she dumped the clothes on the loveseat. "What a load!" she said.

Palmer, Shanon, and Amy stared.

"I told my mom I didn't need all this stuff," the girl explained blithely, "but she's into buying." She stuck her hand out. "Hi, I'm Max Schloss!"

Palmer's mouth dropped open. "*You're* Max Schloss?"

"We thought that Max Schloss was a man or a boy," Amy said, still staring.

"That's what everybody thinks at first," the girl replied. "But as you can see," she added with a grin. "I'm not." In two strides, she reached the doors to the bedrooms. "Where do I sleep?"

"Not in there," blurted out Shanon, pointing to her room. "I mean . . . there's already somebody in there."

"There's somebody in our room, too," volunteered Palmer. She pointed to Amy. "We are."

"You must have come to the wrong place," Shanon volunteered. "This suite is made for four. Are you new at Alma?" she added, trying to be polite.

"I'm a transfer," the redhead explained, sitting down next to her dresses. "Last year I went to a school in New York."

Amy smiled. "New York? That's where I'm from."

10

"What sign are you?" the girl asked eagerly. "My birthday is September 27th, so I'm a Libra!"

"July 16th," Amy said amiably. "That makes me a Cancer."

"I'm from Palm Beach and L.A.," volunteered Palmer. "I'm not sure what my sign is."

"L.A.!" cried the girl. "I go there a lot. Sometimes with my father on location. He's an actor—Maximillian Schloss."

"Maximillian Schloss!" cried Amy. "He's hysterical! I thought your name sounded familiar!"

The girl grinned. "Actually, my full name is Maxine."

"Welcome to Alma Stephens," Shanon said. "Want us to help you find your room?"

"Sure," Max said, standing up. She reached into her jeans pocket. "This is the room assignment they gave me over the telephone." She showed Shanon the piece of paper. *Suite 3-D, Fox Hall* was scrawled across it.

"You must not have heard the right thing over the phone," Shanon said. "This is the wrong place," she repeated as Max's chauffeur brought in a CD player and a trombone case.

"Set the CD down on the table, Ollie," Max instructed.

"Very well, Miss," said the chauffeur. "I'll leave your trombone case over here by the door."

Max smiled. "Thanks for everything, Ollie! See you at Thanksgiving!"

"I think we'd better find your room in a hurry," Shanon said, giggling nervously. Max's stuff was taking over the whole suite. "I wonder who your roommate is, anyway."

"Who's yours?" Max asked innocently.

11

Shanon smiled. "Lisa McGreevy."

"We've had it arranged since last spring," Amy told her.

"Unless," Palmer suggested, "things got mixed up."

Shanon's face flushed. "Mixed up?" she said. "That's ridiculous. Lisa is my roommate, and that's that." She glanced at Max. "No offense, but it was already planned."

"That's okay," said the girl, glancing away. She looked at the slip of paper again. "But where do I . . . ?"

Shanon marched to the door. "I'll go find out for you."

Seconds later, Shanon was standing outside Maggie and Dan's apartment. She knocked softly, then louder. Maggie opened the door, and a small ball of fluff dashed out.

"Not so fast, young lady!" the pretty teacher cried, stooping down to the puppy. She straightened up to greet Shanon. "Hi, there! What do you think of Gracie? Isn't she even cuter than ever?"

"Cuter than ever," Shanon said with a swallow. "I . . . uh, there's a person upstairs in the suite," she stammered.

Dan Griffith stepped up behind Maggie. "What person are you talking about?"

"There's been a mix-up," Shanon explained. "There's someone who says she lives in our suite, and it isn't Lisa."

Maggie touched her arm. "There's isn't a mix-up."

"What do you mean?" Shanon cried. "Lisa and I are supposed to be roommates again. We put in for our assignments last spring. You told us we could—you can't make me live with someone else," she insisted.

"It's a four-person suite," Dan said. "We have to."

"But Lisa is my roommate," Shanon insisted. "Where is *she* supposed to go?"

12

"I'm sorry, Shanon," Maggie said. "I guess you haven't heard."

Shanon blinked. "Heard what?"

"It was a last-minute decision on the part of the Mc-Greevys," Dan explained. "We just found out ourselves. Lisa won't be coming back to Alma this semester."

Shanon's bottom lip began to tremble. She felt as if she were going to be sick. "That's impossible," she declared. "I just got a letter from Lisa. She said she couldn't wait to see me!"

"There's no mistake," Maggie said gently. "Lisa won't be with us this year. Your new roommate is Maxine Schloss."

CHAPTER 2

Dear Shanon,

    By the time you get this letter you will probably know that I'm not coming back to Alma Stephens this year. When I last wrote to you everything was great. As you know, my parents had been having marriage problems, but by the end of the summer they seemed to be getting along fine. Then, suddenly, just before I was supposed to be going back to school, my mom and dad had this terrible argument and my dad left. Just like that! It was horrible, but I'm not quite sure what it means. It probably means that my parents are separated, but I don't understand much of what is going on. Reggie is going back to Ardsley, but I decided right then and there that I wouldn't come back to Alma. There was no way I was going to leave my mother all alone. I've never seen her so upset! The night I told her I didn't want to go back to school, she called my dad and he came over. The three of us had a big talk. They tried and tried to make me go, but I told them no over and over again. How can I leave, knowing that when I come back I may not even have a room anymore? Or maybe not even

14

a mother or a father? Suppose both my parents decide to walk out? Besides, even though they probably don't know it, they really do need me—especially my mom. I have been doing everything I can to make life easier for her. I've had lunch with my dad a few times and am trying to talk him into coming back. I hope it works!

Please don't spread this around. Of course, you can tell Amy and Palmer. I'm not sure I'm going to write Rob about it, though. Last spring I told him that my parents' marriage problems were solved. Now that they are messed up again, it seems kind of embarrassing. I'm planning to keep writing to Rob, even though I might not tell him about my parents right away. He was a great pen pal all summer. Did Mars write to you? How are Amy and Palmer?

Shanon, I really miss you a lot. I'm going to the local public school, which so far seems okay, though I don't have many friends there. I hope whoever your new roommate is, she is a nice person. So long for now. Instead of roommates, at least we can be pen pals. Say hi to everyone!

Love,
Lisa

Shanon swallowed hard. The lump in her throat was so huge she was afraid she might choke. Hot tears welled up in her eyes. It wasn't fair! She and Lisa were supposed to have been roommates forever! Why did Lisa's parents have to have such problems? Why did Lisa have to stay home? Why did things *have* to be different?

"Hi!" Max's voice rang out from the doorway.

Hastily tucking Lisa's letter into her journal, Shanon

15

opened her Latin book. "Hi," she mumbled, darting a glance at her new roommate. As usual, Max Schloss was dressed in bright, clashing colors. This time it was a pink-and-black plaid shirt and a red leather miniskirt. On her feet she wore pink high-top sneakers. Shanon had always heard that as a rule redheads shouldn't wear red or pink. But Max didn't seem to care much about rules.

"I'm trying to decide what to go out for," Max announced, dropping a stack of papers onto the desk. "Do you think you could help me? There's so much to choose from: chorus, orchestra, basketball, *Ledger*—"

Shanon took her eyes off her book. "I don't think they need anyone else on *The Ledger*," she broke in. *The Ledger* was Shanon's main extracurricular activity. It was bad enough living with Max—having to see her all the time in the newspaper office would be unbearable!

Max shrugged. "I wouldn't be much use on a newspaper anyway. I'm not exactly the literary type."

"What type are you?" Shanon asked.

Max picked up her trombone. "The goofy type!" she said, cackling wildly.

Shanon winced. "There are practice rooms in the basement of Thurber Hall," she hinted, "if you want to play your trombone."

"Okay," Max said cheerfully. "Actually, I'm not really into trombone-playing these days. I like science." As the tall girl crossed to the dresser, Shanon observed her out of the corner of her eye. Why did Max wear her hair in such an odd way, she wondered. Instead of wearing one ponytail like most people, Max had her red hair in two ponytails. A little like Pippi Longstocking, thought Shanon. Or maybe a better word to describe it *was* "goofy." In any case, Shanon decided, Lisa would never wear *her* hair like that. Lisa was much more sophisticated.

Max plopped down on her bed and put her feet up. "I hate Latin," she complained with a grin. "I don't think I'm going to like French or English much, either."

"Really?" said Shanon. "Those are my favorite subjects."

"My favorite subjects are chem, bio, and computer science," Max announced, stretching one long leg up toward the ceiling.

"Biology?" Shanon exclaimed. "Ugh! I think cutting up dead animals is horrible."

"I think so, too," Max said, sitting up cross-legged. "But we're talking about cutting up a little frog, not a big animal like Gracie."

Shanon frowned. "Like Gracie?!"

"Just joking," Max said. "She's a cute little mutt."

"She's a Jack Russell terrier," Shanon informed her. "The dorm got her from my mom and dad as a wedding gift for Maggie and Dan last spring." Shanon proceeded to bury her head in her Latin homework.

Max got up and rummaged through a stack of books on the dresser. "What's this?" she asked, picking up a well-worn paperback.

"It's a novel I'm reading," Shanon murmured. "By Michelle Wise, my favorite author."

"Yuk," Max said, putting the book down. "Too romantic. What's this?" she asked, picking up a thin canvas notebook.

Shanon started. "That's my journal!"

"It is?" said Max. "Isn't *that* your journal in front of you?"

17

"Oh, yes," Shanon said, blushing. Clutching her own journal protectively, she stared at the book in Max's hand. "I bought the other one for Lisa," she explained. "It's just been sitting there."

"I noticed," said Max. "Can I have it?"

"What?" Shanon said, feeling flustered. Max Schloss really was pushy!

"I saw that Amy and Palmer have them, too," Max said, "and this one's just lying here. Of course, if you're saving it. . . ."

"No, please take it," Shanon offered, as politely as she could.

"I'll pay you for it," Max said.

"It's okay," Shanon said with an edge. Suddenly the room was beginning to feel uncomfortably small. Couldn't Max see she was busy? And why did her new roommate have to talk so much? Lisa herself had been a great conversationalist, but she wasn't a blabber.

"It's a beautiful day outside. You should take advantage of it and explore the campus," Shanon suggested hopefully.

"Will you go with me?" Max asked.

Shanon blushed. "Well . . . I kind of have things to do," she hedged.

"What?" asked Max. "If it's studying, we can do it together."

"It's not only studying," Shanon told her. She picked up her journal. "It's other stuff. Letters and—"

"If you need stamps, I've got some," Max interjected.

"Thanks," Shanon said, "but I don't." She was hoping Max would leave, but instead, the redhead began to make up her bed. Shanon thought her roommate's Indian-print bedspread looked terrible! It wasn't that the spread itself was so bad. It just didn't go at all with the flowered one on Shanon's bed.

"I have another bedspread in the closet," Shanon said, making a decision. "I was wondering if you would like it."

"Wow," Max cried, jumping to her feet. "That's nice of you. What's it like?"

"Just like mine," Shanon said. "My mother made two of them—one for me and one for Lisa."

Max glanced over at Shanon's bed. "No thanks," she said simply. "I don't like flowered things." She fluttered her bedspread in the air, and the Indian print billowed down over the sheets.

That does it! thought Shanon irritably. Max had just insulted her mother's bedspread! And what kind of person didn't like flowers?! Trying to control her anger, she gathered up her books.

"Ready to go to the library now?" Max asked.

"Yes . . . I mean *no!*" blurted out Shanon. "I—I. . . . Sorry," she stammered. "I just need some privacy."

Max's face reddened. "Sure," she muttered. "I'll make like a salad."

"What did you say?" Shanon asked, bewildered.

Max chuckled. "You know—*Lettuce leaf!* Lettuce-leaf salad, get it? *Let us leave.*"

Shanon forced a laugh. "Oh, yes."

Backing out of the room, Max bumped into her knapsack. "What a klutz I am," she said cheerfully. "See you later. Palmer and Amy are over at the gym. Maybe I'll meet them there."

"I'll see you all later," said Shanon. She could hardly wait for Max to leave.

19

When she heard the front door finally close, Shanon let out a sigh of relief. It was really hard to live with a stranger! Especially a "strange" stranger like Max Schloss. *She isn't anything like Lisa,* Shanon thought wistfully. Lisa had been the perfect roommate. But Maxine Schloss was something else altogether!

Grabbing a piece of paper, Shanon started to write. . . .

Dear Lisa,

To tell the truth, I'm still in a state of shock about your not coming back to Alma. And to make matters worse, my new roommate has got a boy's name. She calls herself goofy, tells corny jokes, hates flowers, and is such a science freak that she actually made a joke about using Gracie in an experiment! I don't know what I'm going to do. I have the feeling this year is going to be horrible—unless you come back to Alma. Maybe your folks don't really need you. Please think about this. I would be the happiest person in the world if you would only come back!

Love,
Your roommate-turned-pen-pal,
Shanon

P.S. My new roommate, who looks like Pippi Longstocking, calls herself Max!

CHAPTER 3

"Isn't this fun!" exclaimed Max, hurrying down the hall behind Shanon, Amy, and Palmer. "Maggie and Dan are *so* neat! It's *so* clever of them to make us all wear hats to the party!"

"It's weird, if you ask me," Palmer said, adjusting her beret. She looked at Maxine's bare head. "And if you think the idea is so clever, how come *you* didn't bring a hat?"

"I did," Max said, pointing to a shopping bag at her side. "I'll put it on when we get there."

A few steps ahead, Amy and Shanon stopped outside the open door of Maggie and Dan's apartment. Other guests had already arrived, and a loud yipping could be heard from inside.

"Just listen to Gracie," Shanon said with a giggle.

"I brought her some dog yummies," said Amy, sticking her hand in a pocket. "I got them at the store when we were in Brighton."

"Nice going," said Shanon.

Like Palmer, Shanon was wearing a beret, but she'd decorated hers with a big feather. Amy had on a baseball cap, backward.

"Come in!" Maggie greeted them warmly at the door.

Shanon, Palmer, and Amy stepped forward, while Max dropped to the rear. "I see you wore your party hats," the French teacher said, adjusting her own jaunty-looking pill-box. "I hope you don't think Dan and I are being silly. We thought it would—" Suddenly Maggie's eyebrows lifted and her mouth dropped open. Shanon, Amy, and Palmer turned around to see what she was staring at. It was Max. The "hat" she'd been carrying in her bag had turned out to be a *big* cooking pot.

"I think we've got an original on our hands, Maggie," Dan announced, coming over to join them. He reached for Max's hand with a friendly smile. "May I show you in? Your bonnet seems to be blocking your vision."

"Thanks," Max replied. From underneath the pot her voice echoed eerily.

Amy, Shanon, and Palmer parted to let Max into the room.

"Good grief," Shanon said. "What a show-off!"

"I think it's funny," said Amy.

"It's *different,* anyway," Palmer said.

After closing the door, the three girls headed straight for the food.

"Maggie's brownies!" Amy cried.

"Aren't they great?" Shanon said, stuffing one in her mouth. "Hey, where are the dog yummies? I want to give some to Gracie."

Plunging her hand into a pocket, Amy came up with some treats. Shanon made her way to the other side of the room.

"Isn't that your sister's roommate?" Amy asked Palmer, glancing at a short, black-haired girl on the couch.

Palmer nodded. "I wonder where Georgette is," she said. "I hope she's not going to be late."

"Is she usually late?" asked Amy.

"Always," Palmer huffed.

On the other side of the room, Shanon had found Gracie. When she held out a treat, the puppy yipped and jumped into her arms. "Hi, Gracie!" Shanon said. "Remember me?"

"She seems to," Brenda Smith answered.

"The smartest thing we ever did was to give Maggie and

Dan a puppy for a gift," Muffin Talbot giggled. "Pets are against the rules for students but not for teachers! At least this way we get to have one in Fox Hall."

Shanon nuzzled the puppy. "That was kind of the idea," she said mischievously as Dan Griffith crossed to the center of the small living room.

"I hate to interrupt," he said in a loud, clear voice, "but I'm going to do it, anyway."

"Great hat, Mr. Griffith!" Gina Hawkins called out.

Dan touched the rim of his old fishing hat. "In case you girls think that Maggie and I have 'lost it,' we haven't. We just wanted an opportunity to welcome you back to Fox Hall and to start off the year with some good fun."

"Not to mention good brownies," Kate Majors said loudly.

There was a sprinkling of laughter.

"If you'll all find seats," Maggie chimed in, "Dan and I would like to share some of our thoughts on what we can all do to make life at Fox Hall even more wonderful this year than last."

Muffin's hand shot up. "May I ask a question first?"

"What is it, Muffin?" said Mr. Griffith.

"If we call Maggie Ms. Grayson-Griffith now that she's married, what do we call you? Mr. Griffith-Grayson?"

"Whatever you like," he said agreeably. "As long as it has the word 'Mr.,' in front of it."

The girls giggled and Gracie barked. Keeping the puppy in her lap, Shanon gave her another treat.

"And now," Mr. Griffith announced, "I'd like to introduce a new upper-former. She's the one in the back row with a pot on her head."

24

All eyes in the room turned to Max, who slowly removed the pot. "Guess I'll take my hat off now," she said nonchalantly.

Several girls in the room burst out laughing. Shanon's face turned red. Why was her roommate acting so silly?

"She's Maximillian Schloss's daughter," Shanon heard Brenda Smith whisper.

"She's a riot," Gina whispered back.

Maggie smiled at Max. "Why don't you stand up and tell us a little bit about yourself?"

As Max stood up and smiled at the group, Shanon noticed that she didn't seem a bit nervous. "Well, some of you have already met me by now," Max said, taking in the crowd, "but I bet none of you know my real name. It's Maxine Edith Schloss. I'm almost fourteen years old and I have three brothers, but I was the oldest, so my dad called me Max and it stuck."

"Is your dad as funny in real life as he is in the movies?" Brenda called out.

Max grinned. "What can I say? He's even nuttier."

Shanon shuddered. It seemed Max would do just about anything for attention, including calling her own father nutty!

"My mom calls me Maxie," the redhead continued, "so if anybody else wants to do that, it's okay. The only other thing I have to say is that I'm glad to be living in Fox Hall and I like my roommate."

Kate whistled and clapped. "Let's hear it for Maxie's roommate!" she cried. "Way to go, Shanon Davis!"

Two pink spots appeared on Shanon's cheeks as the other girls all turned to look at her. Why did Max have to say anything about her? Maybe her roommate liked having

25

that kind of attention, but she certainly didn't!

Shanon breathed a sigh of relief as the door to the apartment creaked open and everyone looked around to see who it was.

"Come in, Georgette," Mr. Griffith's voice boomed across the room. Georgette Durand quietly slipped in. "I was just about to introduce the new third-formers."

"Sorry I'm late," Georgette said. "I was waiting for my sister."

"Waiting for me?" said Palmer. "How come?"

"You said I could come down with you," Georgette whispered. "Remember? You were going to let me borrow a hat. But you were gone when I got to your suite."

"I—I forgot," Palmer stammered. "You still shouldn't have waited," she added. "You—"

"Why don't you girls straighten this out later," Dan's voice interrupted. "There's no problem. Maggie and I were just about to discuss dorm duties. And after that we'll introduce the new girls."

Amy's hand shot up. "I volunteer for leaf-raking detail," she announced.

"You've got it," Maggie said.

"I'll take dog-walking," Max blurted out. The room filled with laughter.

"Is there such a thing as dog-walking?" Muffin asked seriously.

"Not officially," Mr. Griffith replied with a smile. "But if Maxie wants to get up at six-thirty every morning to take Gracie out, I won't stop her."

"Great," said Max. "I'll do it!" She smiled across the room at Gracie and Shanon.

Shanon held the wriggling puppy even closer. Walking

Gracie was something she and Lisa had been planning to do together! But now Max was horning in on it!

"Can there be two people on dog detail?" Shanon asked.

"Sure can!" Max answered for the teacher. "That way I won't disturb you when I get up early."

"Now that that's settled," Mr. Griffith continued, "and before discussing any more work duties, I'd like to ask our new third-formers to please stand up. . . ."

While Georgette and the other new girls introduced themselves, Shanon sat in a corner hardly listening. Ordinarily, she would have been eager to meet the newcomers; she would have listened politely while they spoke and tried to think of something to say to make them feel welcome. But at the moment, she didn't feel at all sociable. Max's show-offy behavior and the way she'd pushed herself into Lisa's dog-walking job were really obnoxious. Max had been at Alma only a few days and already she was taking over! Everybody was laughing at her silly antics and talking about her—probably because her father was a movie star. Last year, Shanon thought sadly, the most popular girl in the dorm had been Lisa. Yet not a single person had asked about her best friend all night. It wasn't fair.

The third-form introductions were brief, and then the two teachers moved on to other dorm business. Further work assignments were made, and the demerit system was reviewed.

"If there's no more business to bring up," Mr. Griffith concluded, "I'd like to—"

"I have something to say," Shanon burst out.

Everyone looked at her.

"What is it, Shanon?" asked Maggie

Shanon stood up, red-faced. "I just wanted to say that I

27

got a letter from Lisa McGreevy and that she says hello to everyone."

"Yaay, Lisa!" exclaimed Kate. Shanon looked out into the room. Though a couple of the other girls smiled, nobody else said a word.

"That's all, I guess," Shanon mumbled as the group broke up and moved toward the refreshment table.

"Help yourself to the brownies!" Maggie called out. "There are more where those came from! And when you leave, please shut the door behind yourselves."

"That's right," Dan boomed above the noise. "We don't want to lose Gracie! And remember—having Gracie upstairs in your rooms is absolutely against policy! We don't want our puppy to get suspended."

Shanon laughed halfheartedly at Dan's joke. Glancing around the room for Gracie, she discovered that Max had already picked up the dog.

"I hear your roommate's father is going to have his own TV series. When does it start?" asked Dawn Hubbard, at Shanon's elbow.

"I don't know," Shanon said. "And I don't care either," she murmured under her breath.

Grabbing a final brownie from the refreshment table, she left the apartment. Looking just as sullen, Palmer followed her out.

"How come you're leaving?" Shanon asked, starting up the stairs with her suitemate close behind.

"Georgette," Palmer said flatly. "Did you hear the way she blamed me for her own lateness?"

"Weren't you supposed to meet her?" Shanon asked.

"Well, yes," Palmer admitted. "But when I wasn't in the suite, she should have known to come down on her own.

28

My stepsister may be brilliant in school, but when it comes to common sense she hasn't got a bit."

"Is Georgette really so smart?" Shanon asked.

"Gifted," Palmer sighed. "That's one of the problems. My dad is always comparing us. He can't understand why I have so much trouble with my grades."

The two girls sat down on the loveseat, and Shanon split her brownie between them. "What should we do now?" she asked glumly.

"I know!" Palmer said, brightening. "Let's write to our pen pals. I haven't written Sam in days."

"I owe Mars a letter, too," said Shanon, "but I'm in such a bad mood I don't think I'd better write him now." She picked up her journal and shot Palmer a mournful glance. "I miss Lisa so much," she said. "Don't you?"

"Sure," Palmer said distractedly. Having selected a piece of pale blue stationery, she was already busy writing to Sam.

She doesn't miss Lisa as much as I do, Shanon thought, crossing to her bedroom. *Nobody does. . . .*

It was just getting dark in Shanon's room, but she didn't turn on the light. Perching on the edge of her bed, she opened her journal. There were already several entries in the new book. She picked up a pen and started to write. . . .

Dear Diary,

I thought that coming back to school would be so much fun, but things are turning out terribly. When you get to know and like somebody a lot, it's hard to lose them the way I lost Lisa. I know I should get over it, but I can't. What's more, I hate my new roommate!

29

CHAPTER 4

Dear Amy,

Greetings! How does it feel to be back at Alma? Life at Ardsley is okay these days. Things look a lot better when you're not a third-former—know what I mean? I cannot tell you how much more respect I am being paid around here. I'm genuinely flattered. As an upperclassman, I no longer have to sit at an assigned seat in the dining hall! Nor do I have only one pass a month to go into Brighton—now I can go any weekend I like! I still have to let people know where I'm going, though. But all I can say is, I'm "flattered." Here's a rap song I wrote in honor of being back in New Hampshire. I hope you like it.

Your pen pal,
John

Back to School, or I'm Flattered,
a rap song by John Adams
Oh, I'm back in town
Kicking up my heels
Be real!

I'm flattered.
Opening up my books
Getting lots of looks,
Baby, what's the deal?
I'm flattered.
Girls, boys, teachers, come up on the sly
Saying, Adams, now you know who's who,
No need to tell me I'm cool
'Cause I know every rule
and all I will say is,
I'm flattered!

Dear John,

All I can say is "I'm *flattered!*" that you sent me this definitely rad rap song. Too bad I can't put it to music. Glad you're feeling okay about being back in school. Same for me! I'm taking voice lessons again with Professor Bernard. I've also been shooting a lot of baskets. Maybe I'll even go out for the team, though my making it would be a "long shot"! (Ha, ha.)

It was great to be back in New York City this summer. Along with all the classes my mom signed me up for, I did a lot of baby-sitting for a five-year-old kid in my apartment building. I spent almost all of the money I made at the record store. I have some dynamite CDs, which I wish I could play for you. Unfortunately, I haven't heard any talk about Alma and Ardsley getting together, at least not over here at Alma. Anyway, as you know, I could never ask you up to our suite. At home in New York, I had my friends over all the time. That's one thing I miss, being back at boarding school. But I agree it is definitely cool being an upper-former. Kate Majors, the dorm monitor, shows us

31

*more respect here also. She's much more liberal about
"lights out" than she was last year. However, no matter
what form we're in, we still have the dress code. You're
lucky you get to wear pants. Skirts are a drag sometimes,
believe me.*

*Well, there's not much else to tell. Except that I am in
advanced math again this year. I'm sure you've heard from
Rob or Reggie that Lisa didn't come back to Alma this
semester. I miss her, but I really like the girl who took her
place. Her name is Maxine, but most people call her Max
and I like to call her Maxie. She is kind of zany, and her
father is an actor who has his own television show coming
on the air soon. Maxie also likes to shoot baskets. I think
you and the other guys would like her.*

Signing off,
Your pen pal,
Amy

P.S. Who is in your suite this year, besides Mars and Rob?

Dear Palmer,

*Welcome back to school. Brighton was not very bright
this summer without you. Please forgive my corny pun, but
I'm writing you after a long, hard day at school and then
band practice. I really appreciated your letters from Palm
Beach and your postcard from L.A. How was your visit
with your father? Did you ever get a job?*

*What classes are you taking this year? I'm starting to
learn Russian. It's a difficult language, but very exciting.
Some other news I want to share is that my band, The
Fantasy, got a second award for our song "Holding
Hands"—this time from the Brighton Chamber of Com-*

merce. Next thing you know we'll be on the Grammys. Joke, joke!

I hope to see you soon. Do you look the same, by the way? The picture I had from last year is getting worn out from my passing it around to people who want to know what my pen pal looks like. Hint, hint! What's new with you? Write soon and take care.

Your pal,
Sam O'Leary

Dear Sam,

Here's a picture that was taken of me this summer. I hope you like it. You can't really see my eyes that well because I'm squinting into the sun. The picture was taken on the beach in Florida—just so you know that I am not frowning. And if you're interested, my eyes are still blue! (Joke.) As far as the rest of my looks are concerned, I'm a little taller and have a suntan. My hair is still blond—I'd never change it. By the way, we've got a super photograph of you in our suite! And I don't mean the one you sent me last year, though that's good, too. Shanon Davis made an enlargement of the group photo that the Foxes had taken with you and our other pen pals last year. Amy says that you and I came out better than anyone else in the picture. Do you remember the day we took it when you were at Alma?

Congratulations on the award that The Fantasy got! I played my dad a tape of you and your band when I saw him over the summer, and I think he was impressed—especially by your drumming. What's new with me is that my courses this year are English, French, math, biology

33

two, Latin, history, music, gym, and art. I still find them kind of hard and boring, except art and gym. Also new is the fact that my stepsister Georgette is at Alma. She is a pain—always blaming me for things she does wrong herself. She's also conceited and brags a lot to people (especially my dad) about how smart she is. Do you like your younger brother?

Thanks for writing.

Yours truly,
Palmer

Dear Shanon,

Greetings from Ardsley Academy! My parrot Ricardo and I are back at Kirby Hall, and glad to be here. Rob is pretty upset about Lisa not being at Alma, though. They're still writing to each other, I think. What was her reason for not coming back, anyway? Rob doesn't seem to know himself. Who took Lisa's place in the Foxes of the Third Dimension? You are still in Suite 3-D, aren't you?

What activities are you going out for? I am lying low for the time being, since my freshman grades weren't satisfactory to my parents. They don't want me too loaded up with extra things. We can't all be brains and super people like you.

How is the puppy you gave to your teachers? I think it was a definitely cool present. As you know, I love animals. In fact, someday I might like to go into the pet business. Maybe I'll open a pet spa or become a veterinarian or even a pet psychiatrist!

Is Alma sponsoring any social functions in the near future? I'd sure like to see you.

The leaves are just turning red—my thing! Autumn, that is—my fav season. Yours is spring, right?

Your ever lovin' "pal,"
Mars

P.S. I don't want to brag, but I grew two inches over the summer! Must be all the vegetables my mother stuffed into me. Simmie Randolph III transferred out of Ardsley this year, so we've got a new guy in our suite! His name is Paul Grant, and he's definitely okay. I think you would like him.

Dear Mars,

It was great to get your letter, I am kind of upset about Lisa not coming back to Alma. I'm sorry for Rob, too, but I can't confide Lisa's reasons for not coming back. I'm sure she'll tell him herself soon. I am glad you like the new person in your suite. My new roommate is kind of wacky: I've tried to get to know her, but it isn't easy. Her dad is that funny actor Maximillian Schloss; her name is Max Schloss.

I cannot wait to see you again since you got taller. I'm a little taller myself. There probably won't be a mixer until Halloween, but I know there's going to be a book fair again this fall and Ardsley will surely be invited to that! So maybe I'll see you then.

Aside from the problem that I'm having adjusting to my new roommate, things are very exciting here at Alma. I have my own column in The Ledger this year! It's the "Leave It to Wanda" column. I can write just about anything I want to, though we try to stick to issues the students think are important. We even have a suggestion box outside the Ledger office where girls can contribute their ideas anonymously. I'm very excited about this. Do you remember my friend Kate Majors? She is the upper-former who dressed up as a refrigerator at the Halloween mixer last year. Anyway, this year she's the editor of the paper. Maybe someday I'll be editor, since writing and literature are my favorite things.

Well, I guess I'll close this letter now. School has just begun, but the homework is already piling up. I have a summer book report due for Mr. Griffith tomorrow. I hardly know what to write about, since I read thirty-four books over the summer. Have you ever heard of Michelle Wise? She writes books for girls my age and is my favorite author. Besides thinking about my book report, I also have to study for a quiz for Maggie Grayson-Griffith's French class. (She got married to Dan Griffith, remember?) So, you can see I have my work cut out for me. As usual, I am dreading art (I cannot draw a straight line) and biology, which is my new roommate Max's favorite subject—she likes cutting up frogs!

Your idea about being a pet psychiatrist is so funny! Would you have a couch for the dogs to lie down on? Maybe I'll send Gracie over to you. Max and I have been walking her every morning. She's a great puppy, but what an ankle-biter! Yesterday, she bit one of my favorite socks and ripped a hole in it! Say "hi" to Ricardo. How is his vocabulary coming along?

Sincerely yours,
Shanon

CHAPTER 5

———◆———

"We really ought to get Maxie a pen pal," said Amy. It was a clear September morning just after gym class and she and Shanon were jogging down by the river.

"What makes you think she'd want a pen pal?" Shanon gasped, out of breath.

"What makes you think she *wouldn't*?" Amy asked, slowing down.

Coming to a sudden stop, Shanon rested her hands on her knees. "I've got a stitch in my side," she complained.

"You're changing the subject," said Amy, tossing her dark head impatiently. "I read Maxie the letter I got from John and she thought it was terrific."

"So what?" said Shanon.

Amy turned and began to jog again. "So I think we ought to get her a pen pal."

"Did she ask you to get her one?" Shanon persisted, struggling to keep up.

"Of course not," Amy replied over her shoulder. "She's probably waiting for us to ask her. After all, she's the newcomer."

"Well, I don't see why we should ask her," Shanon blurted out. "It's me, you, Palmer, and Lisa who started the pen pal exchange. We're the four Foxes of the Third Dimension—aren't we?"

"But Lisa doesn't live with us anymore," Amy pointed out. "And Maxie does."

"That's not the point," Shanon argued. "Lisa's still one of us."

Amy shot Shanon a look. "Let's turn back," she said.

The girls huffed up the hill to the athletic building and headed for the showers.

"Don't go away," Amy said. "I want to talk to you about something." She grabbed a towel and disappeared. As Shanon peeled off her sweats, she could hear Amy singing above the running water. She slipped into the next showerstall.

Minutes later, the two girls met outside in the changing room.

"What do you want to talk about?" Shanon asked, toweling off in front of the locker where her regular clothes were stored.

Amy gave her wet, dark head a vigorous shake. "Maxie," she said.

Shanon turned away and started to dress. Max again!

"I think we ought to try being nicer to her," said Amy.

"We *are* being nice," Shanon said. Avoiding Amy's sharp gaze, she pulled on her green sweater. "You just said you read Max the letter John wrote to you, and yesterday I heard the two of you listening to that *West Side Story* CD together."

"How could you miss it?" Amy said with a chuckle. "We were playing it full volume."

"*I* noticed," Shanon said. "Anyway," she repeated, "we *are* being nice to her."

"Not all of us," said Amy, climbing into her black corduroy skirt. "You don't like her."

"I hardly know her," Shanon said defensively. Picking up her hairbrush, she struggled to untangle a snarl. "I'm still getting used to her."

"I got used to her the first day," Amy said.

"You both come from New York," Shanon pointed out.

"You and Lisa didn't come from the same place, and you got along with her."

Shanon yanked the brush through her hair. "That was different."

Amy frowned. "How come? When you first met Lisa, you had to get to know her. The way you do that is by doing things together. Maxie and I have been shooting baskets."

Shanon sighed in exasperation. "I don't play basketball. And just because you show Max your pen pal letters doesn't mean I have to show her mine! Anyway," she argued, "I do things with her, too. We walk Gracie together every single morning."

Amy looked thoughtful. "I'd forgotten about that. How's it going?"

"Okay, I guess," Shanon muttered. "It would be better if Max wasn't always talking my ear off. All she talks about is how her dad's going to be on television next week."

Amy shrugged. "It must be exciting. Maybe the reason she talks your ear off is because you never talk to her."

"I do find it hard to come up with topics around her," Shanon admitted. "Something about that girl makes me not want to speak. Maybe it's because she brags so much about her father."

"I haven't heard her bragging," Amy said.

"The very first day she told everybody in the dorm who her dad was," Shanon persisted. "And don't forget that snobbish chauffeur she brought with her. To tell the truth, I think she's stuck up."

Amy grabbed her gym bag and slung it over her shoulder. "It isn't like you to have so many opinions about somebody you hardly know," she said. "I don't understand what's going on lately. I've always thought of you as such a nice person."

Shanon blushed in confusion. "And now . . . ?"

"I still like you," said Amy, "but I have to tell you that I think you're being really mean."

"I haven't done anything mean," Shanon said stubbornly.

"It's mean not to give Maxie a chance," said Amy. "I've gotten to know her and I like her a lot."

"Maybe you and I just don't like the same kind of people," Shanon said with a weak smile.

"Of course we do," Amy replied. She put a friendly arm on Shanon's shoulder. "We like each other, don't we? Anyway, you'll never find out whether you like Maxie or not if you don't even try to get to know her."

Shanon sighed. Deep down she knew that Amy was right. "I guess I still miss Lisa," she said.

"We all do," Amy said. And with a toss of her dark hair, she turned toward Thurber Hall. "*Hasta luego,*" she cried. "I've got Spanish now."

*   *   *

40

Later that afternoon, Shanon stopped in at the *Ledger* office to discuss the first issue with Kate Majors.

"I think the headline should be 'Welcome Back to Alma Stephens' or something like that," Kate said excitedly. She pushed up her glasses. "We could do some short pieces on the transfer students, print a list of the new third-form class . . . stuff like that. Of course it has to be entertaining," she added with a chuckle. Then she looked over at Shanon. "You're not listening to me."

Shanon abruptly sat up at her desk. It was true. Her mind had been wandering. "Sorry," she mumbled.

"You've got circles under your eyes," said Kate. "Is anything wrong? You're not sick, are you?" she said, worry in her voice.

Shanon tried to smile. "I'm fine. Just thinking about something."

"Well, I suggest that you start thinking about your 'Leave It to Wanda' column," Kate said, all business again.

"Oh, I have been," Shanon said, perking up. "I'm so happy to have a column of my own. I want the first thing I write to be really humorous."

Kate looked at all the papers on Shanon's desk. "Anything good in the students' suggestion box?" she asked.

"Not yet," Shanon replied. "I guess it's too early. Remember that anonymous gripe we got last year about having 'lights out' too early?" she said. "Dolores wrote a terrific Wanda column on that topic."

Kate chuckled. "Dolores wrote some funny stuff, all right. She was also a good editor."

"Where is she this year?" Shanon asked.

"Princeton," Kate answered.

41

Shanon smiled wistfully. "You must miss her."

"Kind of," Kate said with a shrug, "but I'm glad to have the chance to be the editor."

As Shanon stared out of the window, Kate perched on her desk and said, "I'm sure you must really miss Lisa."

"I do," Shanon admitted. "Are you and Lisa's brother, Reggie, still pen pals?"

"That sort of fizzled out," Kate replied glumly.

Shanon smiled in sympathy. Kate didn't have much luck when it came to boys.

"So, is Lisa what's on your mind?" Kate asked, peering at Shanon through her big horn-rimmed glasses.

"Kind of," said Shanon. "I'm also worried about another person," she hedged. "I think I may have been mean to her . . . without meaning to. I mean, I thought I might hate her, but I'm sure I don't. You see, I haven't really given her a chance," she blurted out. "Do you know what I mean?"

Kate shook her head. "Not really. I've never hated anybody myself. I can't afford to."

Shanon laughed. "Why not?"

"Because everybody hates me," Kate said matter-of-factly.

"No they don't!" Shanon protested. "*I* like you a lot."

"Thanks," Kate said, smiling. "But you know, I'm not exactly Miss Popularity around here."

Shanon dropped her eyes and blushed. She couldn't argue. Not only was Kate naturally kind of bossy, but she was a dorm monitor—a job that didn't help win many friends. Even Shanon hadn't liked Kate much at first, though now she really valued her friendship.

42

"I did hate someone once," Kate announced suddenly.

"Who was it?" asked Shanon.

"My third-form roommate," Kate said, shuffling some papers.

"What did you do?" Shanon asked.

"Slugged it out," Kate answered nonchalantly.

Shanon's big hazel eyes widened in shock. "You mean you hit each other?"

"Of course not." Kate chuckled. "But there was quite a lot of verbal sparring."

Shanon sighed. Verbal sparring was something she didn't like either—in fact, she'd do almost anything to avoid an argument. She'd found her conversation with Amy in the gym really upsetting, and that didn't even count as a real fight.

"So what happened with you and your roommate?" Shanon asked.

"Well, we didn't kill each other."

"What exactly *did* you do?" Shanon prodded.

Kate smiled. "We stuck it out and became friends. Strange, huh?"

After her meeting with Kate, Shanon went to Mr. Griffith's English class. Amy, Palmer, and Max were in the same class, too. Usually Shanon couldn't help staring at her tall, handsome teacher. But today, her gaze kept drifting over to Max. Seated in the third row on the other side of the room, Shanon's tall, red-haired roommate was busily taking notes. She was wearing a lavender blouse, a blue denim skirt, and black cowboy boots. Even though it wasn't the kind of outfit Shanon would ever wear, she had to admit that on Max it looked great. *Amy was right,* Shanon thought: *I haven't been nice to Max.* And if Kate could learn to like a roommate she'd actually started off hating, surely Shanon could learn to get along with one who was just a little weird. She looked across the room again and made a silent vow to herself: No matter how annoying Max seemed at times, and no matter how much she missed Lisa, Shanon was going to be nice to her new roommate.

After English, Shanon dashed after Max. "Going to Booth Hall?" she asked.

Max's green eyes flashed in surprise. "I—I was going to the snack bar," she answered hesitantly.

"Great," said Shanon, keeping pace beside her. "I'll go, too. In fact, I'll buy you a malted."

Max blinked. "Thanks. I don't like malteds, though."

Shanon blushed in confusion. "I'll buy you whatever you *do* like," she said. "Lisa didn't like malteds either," Shanon continued, trying to make conversation. "She preferred shakes and her favorite flavor was chocolate."

"Oh," said Max. "I like strawberry, especially with—"

"Lisa liked strawberry, too," Shanon interrupted.

Once inside Booth Hall, Shanon steered Max toward the bulletin board. "Let's see what's going on," she said enthusiastically.

Max peered at the sign of the fall book fair. "What's that?" she asked.

"It's a fair where the school sells books," Shanon explained. "There's a volunteer list if you want to help," she added. "Let's both put our names down."

"Okay," Max said, "but I'm not sure I—"

44

"Lisa and I did this last year," Shanon cut her off again, hastily scribbling her name and Max's on the list. "I'll tell you what to do. Don't worry."

Max gave her a puzzled look. "Thanks. I'm trying out for the basketball—"

"The basketball team?" Shanon picked up. "Lisa went out for crew."

"Crew's nice, too," Max said, trying to be agreeable.

On the way into the snack bar, the two girls bumped into Brenda Smith and Gina Hawkins. "When is your dad's show going to air?" Brenda greeted Max, who couldn't seem to remember the exact date.

"I read in a magazine that his routine's more slapstick than ever," piped up Gina.

"Weirder than ever," Max said, laughing. "We're a family of wackoes."

Brenda and Gina went away giggling.

"The TV show sounds very exciting," Shanon bubbled, hardly looking at Max. "You must be really proud of your dad."

"I guess so," Max said quietly.

Shanon glanced at her roommate. Instead of her usual "up" expression, Max was wearing a pensive frown.

"To tell the truth," Max said, "it's kind of embarrassing. I'm not sure I'm so anxious to see my fa—"

"Oh, come on—I'm sure you're anxious to see your father on television!" Shanon exclaimed, only half-listening to Max. The waitress came over. "We'll have a strawberry shake and a chocolate malted," she said.

"It's nice of you to treat me," Max said, suddenly looking happy again.

"That's okay," Shanon said, feeling pretty good herself. "Lisa and I always used to treat each other. I wrote to her about you."

Max blushed. "You did?"

"Now that we're not roommates, Lisa and I are pen pals," Shanon explained. "Mars is my pen pal, too."

"Amy told me about her pen pal, John," Max said.

"Lisa had a pen pal, too," Shanon continued. "Rob Williams. He's really cute. At least Lisa thinks so."

The waitress brought their order, and for a moment the two girls drank in silence. Shanon thought things were going pretty well.

"I really shouldn't eat chocolate," she said, keeping up the conversation, "but with Lisa around I got into the habit. It's amazing how she can eat whatever she likes and never get pimples."

"Lucky," Max grunted. "Not only do I get pimples, I put on weight."

"Me, too," said Shanon. "So does Lisa. But even when she gains, she still looks perfect."

Max stared at Shanon for a moment. Then she let out a sigh. "I hope you don't mind my saying this," she said, "but could we please talk about something else?"

Shanon's face got hot. "What do you mean?"

Max shrugged. "It's just that . . . I'm sure Lisa is a great person, but enough is enough."

"Gosh," Shanon gulped. "Was I talking about Lisa a lot?"

Max nodded. "She does sound perfect."

"I didn't mean to take over the conversation," Shanon said, embarrassed. "It's just that Lisa and I—"

Suddenly Max tipped over her milkshake. "What a klutz!" she muttered, reddening. "Sorry," she said, sopping up the mess.

"There wasn't much left in it anyway," Shanon said sympathetically.

Max grinned. "I'm always spilling things. A total klutz," she repeated.

Shanon glanced at the stain on the table and slurped the end of her malted. There was a long silence, and Shanon began to feel self-conscious. If she couldn't talk about Lisa, what else was there to say?

"Tell me more about the book fair," Max suggested as if she had just read Shanon's mind. "I hope it's not going to be boring."

"It couldn't possibly be boring," said Shanon. "Books are so wonderful."

"That Michelle Wise book of yours wasn't too exciting," Max volunteered. "I read the first couple of chapters."

"I'm sure you would have liked it if you bothered to finish it," Shanon snapped. She still wanted to be nice to Max, but she wasn't about to let anybody criticize her favorite author.

"I don't really like that kind of literature," explained Max. "I prefer science fiction."

"Science fiction?" Shanon gasped. "That's so childish."

"No, it's fun," Max protested. "In fact, I went to a book fair once where they had a science-fiction table and the people selling the books were dressed up as aliens."

Shanon wrinkled her nose. "It sounds silly to me."

"I didn't think so," huffed Max. "It was fun."

"Well, we've never had that kind of book fair at Alma," Shanon informed her. "Elaine Jones, the librarian here, likes serious literature."

"Michelle Wise isn't serious literature," Max pointed out. "She writes pop fiction."

"What difference does it make?" Shanon snapped. "Mrs. Jones isn't going to go for science fiction, and that's that."

Max shrugged. "I'm on the committee. I'll ask her."

"And I'll ask her about the books I'm interested in," declared Shanon.

The two girls turned angry eyes on each other, then looked away.

"See you later," Max finally said.

"Back at the suite," Shanon added, trying to sound cheerful. "Maybe we could walk Gracie an extra time?" she suggested, forcing a smile.

"How about taking her up to our room and playing with her for a while?" Max asked.

"That's against the rules," Shanon reminded her. "Of course, Lisa and I used to break rules sometimes," she added with a chuckle. "We used to raid the kitch—"

Max turned away abruptly, and Shanon let out a sigh. She'd tried. She really had.

CHAPTER 6

That evening, as Palmer, Shanon, and Amy were studying in their suite, Amy suddenly looked up and asked, "Where's Maxie?"

"I saw her with Brenda and Muffin and a bunch of other people after dinner," Palmer said stretching out on the loveseat. "They were all talking about her father's new show. The premiere is Thursday night."

"I know," Amy said excitedly. "As soon as Maxie gets back, I want to ask about getting her a pen pal. I bet lots of boys would be interested in writing to the daughter of a famous TV star."

Shanon looked up from her notebook. "I had a talk with Max this afternoon," she said quietly. "I was trying to be nicer, like you suggested."

"How did it go?" Amy asked.

"I'm not sure," Shanon hedged. She could feel her cheeks getting warm. "I kind of got the feeling Max doesn't like me."

"How could anybody not like you?" Palmer asked.

"You're such a nice person." Smiling, she picked up her French text. "How about it? Will you help me with my homework?"

"Flattery will get you everywhere," Shanon chuckled, taking out her French vocabulary list.

"I want to know what Maxie said to make you think she doesn't like you," Amy persisted. "Maxie is a really outgoing person. I'm sure she likes everyone."

Shanon shrugged. "She doesn't like my taste in books and she doesn't like me to talk about Lisa."

Amy frowned. "Well, I certainly hope that you and Maxie hit it off soon. We all have to live with each other. We—" She broke off abruptly as the door swung open, but it wasn't Max—it was Georgette Durand. She was holding a sheet of notebook paper in one hand and a pale blue sweater in the other. "Hi, everybody!" she said, not waiting to be asked in. Crossing quickly to the loveseat, she held the sweater out to Palmer. "Here's your sweater," she said.

"Where did you get it?" Palmer asked in surprise.

Georgette smiled. "I kind of borrowed it. I was wearing it all day. Didn't you notice?"

"Of course I noticed," Palmer grumbled. "I figured you had one just like mine. And the next time you want to borrow something, please ask."

"Okay," Georgette said with a shrug. Then she handed Palmer the sheet of paper. "Here's your book report."

"What are you doing with that?" Palmer exclaimed, snatching the paper away.

"I saw it on your desk when I was in here borrowing the sweater," Georgette announced, smiling. "It's pretty good. I just corrected the misspellings."

50

"Thank you very much," Palmer said coldly. "Anything else?"

"No, that's all." Georgette smiled and waved at Shanon and Amy. "See you around, guys," she said.

"Aargh!" Palmer screeched as soon as Georgette was out the door. "What a pest! What a brat!"

"I think she means well," Shanon said. "She was trying to be nice."

"You call sneaking in and taking my sweater nice?" sputtered Palmer. "Not only that, she practically said I was stupid!"

"How?" Amy said with a chuckle. "By correcting your spelling?"

"I didn't ask her to correct my book report," fumed Palmer. "I didn't ask her to come to Alma Stephens!"

"Maybe you should be nicer to her," Shanon suggested, remembering her talk with Amy about Max. "Maybe if you did some things together with her you'd get along better."

"Maybe we could get *her* a pen pal," said Amy.

"No way!" said Palmer. "If we get Georgette a pen pal, it'll only give her an excuse to hang around here. It's hard enough having her in the same dorm."

"Okay," said Amy, "she's *your* sister. But we're definitely getting Maxie a pen pal."

"That's different," Palmer allowed. "Max lives right here in Suite 3-D with us. Technically, she's a Fox of the Third Dimension."

"My sentiments exactly," Amy said. She glanced at Shanon. "Right?"

"Sure," Shanon said, determined to be a good sport. "Lisa isn't here anymore, and Max is."

"This is so exciting," said Palmer, grabbing her notebook. "If we're getting Max a pen pal, we can run a whole new ad in the Ardsley *Lion*! Maybe we should put something in the ad about ourselves."

"Like what?" Amy said curiously.

Palmer pursed her lips. "Like 'Elite group of four gorgeous girls in need of one extra boy pen pal . . . etc., etc.' What do you think?" she asked, flashing a smile.

"I think it makes us sound like a club," said Amy. "We're not an elite group. We're just suitemates."

"We are a group," Palmer argued. "We're the Foxes of the Third Dimension. No one else calls themselves that. We're the ones who started people advertising for boy pen pals."

"Still," said Shanon, "if we want to get a pen pal for Max, we should say something about her, not about us."

"I agree," said Amy. "Maybe we should describe her."

"We'd have to say she's a giant," Palmer giggled. "Max is the tallest girl I've ever known. We'll have to find a boy at least her size."

"And he'll have to have original taste in clothes," Shanon added. "I've never seen anybody who dresses like Max."

Amy nodded. "I think she shops a lot in the New York thrift shops. They sell all kinds of weird stuff there. Maybe we can get her a musical pen pal," she continued.

"I never heard of a *girl* trombone-player before," Palmer chimed in.

"It's an unusual choice," Amy said approvingly. "But Maxie's unusual all around. I've never known anybody who can talk for as long as she can."

"She should join the debate team," Palmer said.

"She'd have them rolling in the aisles with all those corny jokes she tells," Shanon said with a giggle. "Have you noticed how often she spills things?" she added curiously. "For someone who looks so graceful, she's a real klutz."

"Even she says so," Palmer said, laughing. "Why, I bet she—" Palmer stopped short as the sitting-room door opened and closed with a bang.

"Hi, Maxie," Amy said, getting up. "Where have you been?"

"In the common room," Max said flatly.

"We were just talking about how we wanted you to have a pen pal just like we do," Amy explained with a smile.

Without smiling back, Max brushed past her.

"It'll be fun," Shanon encouraged. "We've really enjoyed writing to Mars, John, and Sam. And I know that Rob and Lis—" She cut herself off, then finished hastily: "I mean, we'd really like you to do the same thing."

Max gave Shanon a sharp look, then lowered her eyes. "I can't talk about this now," she said. "I have to study."

"Can't you just tell us yes or no?" Palmer insisted. "It's a sure way of having dates. And look how cute our pen pals are," she added, pointing to the group photo.

Max glanced at the picture on the bookcase. "Nice," she said. "I guess the girl on the end is Lisa."

"She's the one in the red turtleneck," Amy piped up.

All three girls looked at Max expectantly.

"I'm not interested," she mumbled. "Excuse me. . . ." And with that, she strode into her bedroom and shut the door firmly behind her.

"Gosh," said Amy, "what a shame."

"She's not interested in having a pen pal?" Palmer said in amazement. "Maybe she doesn't like boys?"

"I think it's because of me," Shanon said in a low voice.

"What does any of this have to do with you?" Amy demanded.

"Max doesn't like me," Shanon explained. "She doesn't want to do any of the things I do—including having a pen pal."

"Maybe she doesn't want to do the things *any* of us do," Palmer suggested, glancing at the door.

"Too bad," Amy said wistfully. "It would have been fun. . . ."

On the other side of the door, Max was fighting back tears. Before she'd entered the room, she'd heard everything Shanon, Amy, and Palmer said through the closed door. Now she knew what they really thought of her! It was bad enough that Shanon had treated her like poison from the very first minute they'd met. Max knew she could never take Lisa's place in Suite 3-D. But to hear all three of the girls talking about her behind her back! It was horrible. They'd called her a giant, a klutz, and a weirdo all in one sitting! They'd said she talked too much, told corny jokes, and played a *boy's* musical instrument! Max sighed with misery. Of course, she'd always known she was different. How many girls had a dad who made his living acting like a nut—in front of millions of people?! But when it came to weirdness, she couldn't blame everything on him. *Palmer was right,* she thought grimly, *I am a giant! And my hair is totally ridiculous!*

No one had said a single thing that wasn't true, Max decided. At least her suitemates were being honest. But why, then, when she came into the room had they made believe they were glad to see her? And why had Shanon been pretending to like her that afternoon in the snack bar? Probably the only reason her suitemates had suggested getting a pen pal was to make up for the mean way they'd treated her. Maybe not Amy, Max decided, but Shanon certainly. Shanon probably hadn't wanted her to have a pen pal at all! Max figured that Amy must have talked her into it.

Wiping her eyes with her shirtsleeve, Max picked up her journal to write:

Entry in Max Schloss's Journal—Tuesday
Today was just as bad as all the other days since I've been at Alma Stephens. I still don't have any friends, except maybe Amy. But I'm not Amy's best friend, since she has to be loyal to Palmer and to Shanon, who I'm sure don't like me. To make things worse, everybody else in the dorm keeps asking me all the time about my father. Isn't there anything else about me they think is worth knowing?

I thought Shanon Davis was going to be a great person to live with, but now I can see that she's really stuck up. If she doesn't want to be my friend, I won't try to be hers. I really feel lonely. It's the pits being a newcomer.

CHAPTER 7

———◆———

"Jeune!" Shanon called out.

"Uh . . . *young?*" Palmer guessed.

"Great," said Shanon.

"Yeah, great," Palmer muttered, resting her head on her elbow. The two girls were eating their lunch in the dining hall. "Now if I can only remember how to spell *jeune* on the next French test," sighed Palmer.

"Greetings," Amy called, joining them at the center table they always chose. "As you can see," she said, glancing at a stack of mail on her tray, "I made a stop at the mailboxes. We hit the jackpot," she added with a grin.

"Letters!" squealed Palmer with an exaggerated French accent. She grabbed the mail and began riffling through it. "That's a word I know in any language."

"Thanks for checking my box, Amy," Shanon said with a smile. "Anything for me?" she asked Palmer.

"Two!" Palmer announced. "This one's from Lisa. I can tell by the handwriting."

"Lisa!" Shanon gasped, reaching for a pink envelope. "It's been so long since she's written."

"And this one seems to be from Mars," Palmer said, handing over a second, gray envelope.

Shanon blushed with pleasure. "Gosh, I did hit the jackpot."

"So did I," said Palmer. "I got a letter from Sam."

"And I got one from John," Amy said cheerfully. "I thought I'd wait to open it when you two opened yours."

Palmer munched a carrot stick. "Who's going to go first?" she asked, picking up Sam's letter and giving it a sniff. "Sam used those fragrance markers again."

"What does his letter smell like this time?" Amy asked, raising one dark eyebrow.

Palmer giggled. "Vanilla."

Shanon picked up the pink envelope. "I think we really should read this one first. Poor Lisa . . ." she murmured. "The last time I heard from her, her dad had moved out."

"I know what that's like," Palmer commiserated. "Tough break."

"Hey, look who's here," Amy said brightly.

Shanon shifted her eyes to the door.

"Hey, Maxie!" Amy called out.

Max waved from the door, then sat down with Gina and Muffin at a nearby table.

"I guess she doesn't want to eat with us," Amy said, disappointed. "I asked her to shoot baskets yesterday, but she said she didn't have time."

"I guess she doesn't like you, either," Shanon said.

"Will you stop saying that Maxie doesn't like us," Amy said with an edge in her tone. "She's just been too busy to hang out with me, that's all."

"I hope you're right," Shanon said. "But as far as I can tell, she acts like she hates us. She hardly ever speaks to me anymore, even when we're walking Gracie together."

"That *is* a switch," said Palmer. "Max is always so talkative."

"Not anymore," Amy admitted. "She's different now. I've noticed it, too. I wonder what's bothering her."

There was a burst of laughter from Max, Muffin, and Gina's table.

"Tell us some more about your dad!" the Foxes heard Muffin squeal.

Shanon rolled her eyes. "She's talking about her father again. It doesn't sound as if anything's bothering her now."

"Read Lisa's letter," Palmer prodded. "I want to get it over with so I can read Sam's."

"All right," Shanon agreed, opening the pink envelope. While Palmer and Amy began eating, she read Lisa's short letter out loud.

Dear Shanon,

Sorry I haven't written. I've been too busy. Chestnut High is great! I have a new friend named Betsy—and there are tons of boys here! How are you? Your new roommate doesn't sound too bad. Maybe you should try to get used to her. After all, you're going to be living together for a long time.

Bye for now,
Lisa

"Gosh," said Shanon in surprise, "Lisa doesn't sound as if she misses us at all."

"She sounds as if she's having fun," Amy said.

58

"She didn't even mention her parents' separation," Palmer pointed out. "Maybe they got back together!"

"Or maybe Lisa is so busy with all those boys at Chestnut High that she doesn't have time to think about her parents," Amy added.

"Maybe she's too busy with her friend Betsy," Shanon said crossly.

Amy gave her a questioning look. "Aren't you glad Lisa's got a new friend?"

Shanon hung her head. "Sure I am. It's just that all this time I was thinking that Lisa was miserable. And I've missed her so much. I just thought that maybe . . . she missed me, too."

"She probably does," said Amy.

"I hope so," said Shanon. "It sounds as if she has a new best friend."

"For heaven's sake!" Palmer said, rolling her eyes. "People can have more than one best friend. I've got tons of them," she added as Georgette suddenly appeared at the table.

"Hi," Georgette said, handing her stepsister a stamp-sized red book. "I got you a present."

Palmer blinked. "You got me a present?" She peered at the book. "What is it?"

"A miniature French dictionary," Georgette said. "I figured if you have as many problems spelling in French as you do in English, you could use it."

Palmer's face dropped. "Thanks," she said dully. "I guess a bad speller like me can use all the dictionaries she can get."

"You're welcome," said Georgette. "That's what I

thought." She eyed an empty seat at the table. "Can I sit there?"

Palmer looked away. "We're kind of busy."

Georgette's eyes narrowed. "I had a feeling you'd say that. I can take a hint. Guess I'll go join my boring roommate."

"That was really mean," Amy said after Georgette had crossed the room to join Tina Penderhew.

"I think so, too," Palmer whined. "Imagine her giving me a French dictionary. It's obvious she thinks I'm a real dummy."

Amy's mouth dropped open. "*You* were the one who was mean, not Georgette. You practically told her to drop dead when she asked to sit down."

"I'm afraid that's what it seemed like, Palmer," Shanon added.

Palmer darted a guilty look in her stepsister's direction and then picked up her letter from Sam. "I have a perfect right to some privacy with my friends," she said defiantly. "If I'm going to read my letter from Sam, I don't want Georgette hanging around." And ripping open the vanilla-scented envelope, she started to read:

Dear Palmer,

Thank you for the picture of yourself at the beach. It's great!!! Hope to see you soon in person. We are working on Shakespeare in English. I really like the guy's style. I am thinking of putting some of his words to music. What do you think? As for your difficulties with your sister, I don't have too much to say except that my younger brother is sometimes a pain but I like him anyway. Did I tell you that I'm still working at Figaro's Pizza as a bicycle messenger?

60

I decided not to go back to Suzy's Shoe Emporium. So, if you ever happen to stop in at Figaro's, you might just see me.

> *Sincerely,*
> *Sam*

"He thinks my picture is great," Palmer said gaily. "And he's working at Figaro's. The next time I get a town pass, I'm definitely going to drop by."

"Sounds good," said Amy. "I'd love a slice of one of Figaro's Monstro pizzas. Meanwhile. . . ." She opened John's letter:

Dear Amy,
> *A dream*
> *There was a house that I thought was small*
> *Only in my dream it was larger*
> *I am capable of great things, I think,*
> *But then I remember the dinosaurs!*

"John's letters are hard to understand," Shanon said.

"I'll say," Amy agreed with pride. "They're like riddles."

"Maybe he's talking about how the dinosaurs became extinct," Palmer suggested. "Maybe he thinks that human beings are going to be extinct, too."

"I'll have to think about that," said Amy. She tapped Shanon's arm. "Read your letter from Mars."

Shanon opened Mars's letter:

Hello, Senorita,
> *Guess what? I've got a great new project. I'm tutoring a*

third-grade class in beginning Spanish at the Brighton Library. I read these very simple books in Spanish to them and they really like it! It's all part of the Ardsley Big Brother program. This is one extracurricular project my parents approve of. Ricardo can now say hola!, *which means "hello" in Spanish. Sorry things are not going well with your new roommate. Somebody here who knows her says Max Schloss is a very nice person. Maybe you should give her another chance before you decide not to like her. Greetings to all the Foxes (is Max a Fox, too, now?).*

Love,
Mars

"Interesting," Amy murmured.

"His parrot speaks Spanish!" exclaimed Palmer.

"He also knows somebody who knows Maxie," Amy pointed out.

"And that person thinks Max is a nice person . . ." Shanon said. She glanced over at the redhead's table. She was still sitting with the two other girls. "It's Max's choice if she doesn't want to be friends with us," she said stubbornly. "I gave her a chance like Mars said I should. I already tried."

"Reading your pen-pal mail, huh?"

Shanon, Amy, and Palmer turned to find Kate Majors standing near the table.

"You might want to read this, too, while you're at it," Kate said, handing Shanon a note. "I found it in the 'Leave It to Wanda' suggestion box."

"Neat!" said Shanon. "It's our first idea of the year!"

"It's hot," Kate said with a nod. "You should definitely consider it."

"What does it say?" Amy asked Shanon.

" 'Leave It to Wanda' is a great column," Palmer chimed in.

Shanon scanned the note in bewilderment. "It's strange."

"What does it say?" Amy wanted to know. "Did somebody complain about the dress code? I wish! Maybe you can write a funny column about Wanda wearing jeans to class."

"It isn't about the dress code," Shanon said in alarm. "It's about a group of girls in Fox Hall."

"Fox Hall?" said Palmer. "Let's see it."

"Let me see, too," Amy said, crowding over.

The brief note was typewritten on a sheet of notebook paper. Palmer and Amy read it together.

If you want an idea for the "Leave It to Wanda" column, maybe you should write about how bunches of girls are mean to other girls who are just trying to make friends. I live in Fox Hall, and I'm new to the school. There is a group of girls who are acting snobby to me—they're what you would call a clique. How do I get to be friends with them?

Signed,
An anonymous newcomer

"Yuk," Palmer said, dropping the note. "That's not a suggestion, that's hate mail!"

"Whoever wrote it sounds angry," Amy agreed.

"Or hurt," Shanon said quietly.

She glanced over at the table where Max had been sitting with Gina and Muffin. The other two girls had left, and

63

Shanon's roommate was sitting alone. "I wonder who could have written this?" Shanon asked with a gulp.

"Yes, who wrote it?" Amy echoed. "And who are the snobby girls this person is talking about?"

Palmer swallowed. "I hope it isn't us."

"Of course it's not *us*." Amy snorted. "We're not a bunch of snobs!"

"We *are* kind of a group," Shanon admitted, shame-faced.

"An elite group," Palmer said weakly. "We even have a code name."

"That's the silliest idea I've ever heard," Amy said. *"I'm* not a snob and I know it! And as for this note," she said, flipping the piece of paper over, "it's probably somebody's idea of a joke. And I have no time for jokes. I'd better hurry now or I'll be late for my lesson with Professor Bernard."

"I've got to go to the art studio," Palmer said, beginning to slink out after Amy.

Shanon fiddled with her fork. "I'll see you later," she said glumly.

As soon as Amy and Palmer were gone, Shanon looked at the note again and felt her face flush. If there was one thing that she liked about Alma Stephens it was the fact that so many different kinds of girls went there. Social clubs and sororities were even against the rules. That snobby bunch of girls couldn't be the Foxes, she thought. Or could it?

Shanon got up and hastily put back her tray. Max was still all alone at her table, reading a book. *What an awful year!* thought Shanon. She and Max were roommates and hardly speaking to each other. And meanwhile Lisa was

64

having no trouble at all finding a new friend. Shanon thought again of Mars's letter. Maybe she *hadn't* tried hard enough to get to know Max. Maybe she would just have to try again.

CHAPTER 8

Palmer knocked on Georgette's door. *Maybe Amy was right,* she thought. Maybe she had been too mean to Georgette. Instead of putting her down by giving her the French dictionary, her stepsister might actually have been trying to help. Besides, the letter in the "Leave It to Wanda" box had really hit home. Even if the note wasn't about the Foxes, Palmer knew she'd definitely been snobbish to Georgette—on purpose! Every time her stepsister came around, Palmer had managed to be too busy with the Foxes.

It really was strange, Palmer mused. She and her stepsister had never gotten along—not even when they were little. Palmer just plain didn't like her. And yet, suddenly, and for no good reason, Palmer felt vaguely guilty as she waited outside Georgette's room.

Georgette opened the door. The petite blonde looked surprised to see her, and Palmer realized that in all the weeks her stepsister had been in Fox Hall, this was the first time she'd visited her.

"Come in," Georgette said, opening the door wider. Un-

66

like the Foxes, who'd been lucky enough to draw a spacious suite their first year at Alma, Georgette and her roommate lived in a cramped double with no sitting room.

Tina Penderhew looked up from the desk where she was studying. "Hope I'm not disturbing anybody," Palmer said.

"It's okay," Tina said, getting up. "I was just about to go to the library." She picked up her books and smiled. "See you later, Georgie!" she called on the way out.

"Georgie?" Palmer giggled as the door banged shut behind Tina.

Georgette rolled her eyes. "What can I say? The girl's a total dweeb. I've told her a thousand times not to call me that. Sit down," she told Palmer, stretching out on her pink bedspread.

Palmer perched on the other bed. Tina's sheets and spread were blue with pictures of wide-eyed kittens on them. "Nice sheets," Palmer quipped, trying to make conversation.

Georgette rolled her eyes. "Truly juvenile."

The two girls giggled uncomfortably.

"Thanks for the French dictionary," Palmer blurted out.

"Do you really like it?" Georgette asked.

Palmer shrugged. "I'm sure I'll find some use for it." She eyed Georgette's open closet. "You've got a lot of new stuff in there."

"Daddy said I could spend whatever I wanted," Georgette announced blithely.

Palmer bristled. Her father had put a definite ceiling on her own clothing allowance this year. "Goody for you," Palmer said, forcing a smile. "He took *my* charge card away."

"That's because you spent too much last year," Georgette pointed out. "This is the first time I've ever had a charge card. And even though he said I could spend as much as I want, I know there's a limit."

Palmer had to chuckle. "I guess I *did* go a little bit overboard ordering things from catalogues," she admitted. "Last spring I got twelve different outfits at once—just so I could try them on. I ended up giving most of the stuff to Amy, Shanon, and Lisa."

"See what I mean?" said Georgette. "I'm sure Daddy will give you your charge card back soon. That is, when he thinks you're more responsible."

"I'm sure he will," Palmer muttered, stifling her irritation. Why did Georgette have to follow up everything with an insult?

"Of course I would have done the same thing if I hadn't been able to learn from your mistake," Georgette went on, flashing an impish grin.

Palmer blinked. "You mean you're acting responsible just because *I* got in trouble? You wouldn't have been that way all by yourself?"

"Of course not, silly," said Georgette. "Younger siblings often learn from the mistakes of the older children in the family. Anybody who knows their child psychology knows that."

Palmer sighed. Her kid sister was way ahead of her. Palmer wasn't sure she could even spell the word *psychology*, let alone understand anything about it. "I know we've always fought a lot," she said, walking over to the window and staring out, "but that's *our* business—right?"

"Sure," Georgette said with a shrug.

"You wouldn't do something jerky like complain about

68

me and my friends to the newspaper, would you?" Palmer asked.

Georgette let out a peal of laughter. "To the newspaper? Don't be ridiculous! Why would I do something like that?"

"I—I guess you wouldn't," Palmer stammered. "Just checking. . . ." She headed toward the door.

"Hey, wait," Georgette called out. Palmer turned back to face her. "I haven't been to Brighton yet," the younger girl said hesitantly. "I was wondering . . . if you . . . ?"

"You want me to take you to town this Saturday?" Palmer said with magnanimity. "Sure. We'll stop at Figaro's Pizza and I'll introduce you to Sam O'Leary."

"You will?" Georgette exclaimed. "That's great! Thanks a lot!"

The two sisters locked eyes. Georgette looked so happy; it was almost embarrassing. "We can do some shopping, too," Palmer offered on an impulse.

"You won't forget, will you?" said Georgette.

Palmer smiled. "'No, I won't forget. I promise."

Georgette averted her eyes. She was silent for a long moment. "Maybe I should tell you something," she said quietly.

"What is it?" asked Palmer.

"Oh . . . oh, nothing. . . ." Georgette tossed her head, then smiled at Palmer. "See you later, Sis!" she exclaimed.

Palmer's eyes widened. Georgette had never called her *that* before. It sounded kind of nice. "Okay," she said, smiling back.

Palmer was still smiling as she headed back to Suite 3-D. Her conversation with Georgette had definitely made her feel better. Now, whatever Amy thought, Palmer knew for sure that *she* wasn't mean. *Having a stepsister at school might not be so bad after all,* she thought. She and Georgette were the only kids in the family. It would be nice if they could be friends, too.

"Your hair looks great that way," Shanon said, fishing for something nice to say as Max stood in front of the mirror, brushing her thick mane.

"If you like the lioness look," Max muttered, sticking on a headband. Without glancing at Shanon, she walked to the closet.

"I wanted to talk to you at lunch . . ." Shanon began hesitantly.

"You did?" Max said with a sharp look.

". . . but you were sitting with so many other people," Shanon went on. Her voice trailed off again. It wasn't easy talking to her roommate. Max was making it really obvious that she didn't like her!

Max pulled on her boots. "My dad's TV show premieres tonight," she mumbled. "Everybody's excited about it."

Shanon smiled. "You must be, too!"

Max swallowed and bit her lip. Actually, "excited" wasn't the word for her feelings. She was feeling both embarrassed and scared. Her father's acting was great, but this television show sounded totally slapstick. "I hope he's not *too* wild," she blurted out with a self-conscious chuckle.

"I'm sure he will be," Shanon said, trying to be friendly. "After all, he's a comedian."

Max reddened. How could she expect Shanon Davis to understand her feelings? Shanon, who'd hardly bothered to get to know her? Besides, it was obvious that Shanon really disliked her.

70

"I was going to invite you to come to my house for the weekend," Shanon said, standing up.

"You were?" Max asked in surprise.

"I'm going to invite Amy and Palmer," Shanon added hastily, "and I'm sure they'll come so I thought I should—"

Max turned away to hide her disappointment. For a moment she had thought Shanon might have actually changed her mind about her. But it was clear Shanon was only trying to be polite.

Shanon blushed. Max didn't look at all interested. "I guess you think it would be . . . boring," she stammered.

"I'll just be too busy to go," Max said coolly.

"It's my grandmother's seventieth birthday," Shanon said, trying to persuade her. "My mom's making a big cake. Our house is fun—really! Last year Lisa and—"

Max turned away, no longer listening to Shanon. She had something more important to worry about—her dad's show!

"Sorry," Shanon said quickly. She hadn't meant to bring Lisa's name up again.

But Max was already on her way out the door.

"I can't talk now," Max said, heading downstairs.

Shanon followed, determined to be friendly, no matter what. "Is it time for the show?" she asked. "Mind if I come along, too?"

"It's a free country," Max muttered. She glanced at Shanon. Having her roommate watch her dad's show might be embarrassing. Suppose he messed up and wasn't funny? "My dad can be kind of weird," she warned. "You may not like the show at all."

"Oh, I've heard he's sensational!" Shanon bubbled.

"Thanks," said Max, "but you don't have to say that."

71

"I'm just trying to be friendly," Shanon pressed.

"How come?" Max asked. "I know you don't like me," she said in a loud voice as they reached the bottom of the stairs. Inside the common room, the television was blaring.

"I do like you," Shanon protested, "I mean, there was a time—but now I'm trying—"

"Well, you can stop trying," Max said. "And there's no need to apologize because I feel the same way about you." She darted a nervous look into the big room, then stepped back into a corner of the lobby. Shanon just stared at her. "And if you think *I'm* strange," Maxie went on sarcastically, "you don't know the meaning of the word. Just wait until you see my dad!"

"Hey, Maxie!" yelled Muffin. "What are you waiting for? Come on in. Your dad's show is starting!"

"Hurry up or you'll miss it!" called Gina.

Joining the other girls in the common room, Max left her roommate standing in the doorway. Shanon felt stung by Max's anger—this time she had really been trying to be her friend! But Max kept treating her like poison.

Shanon waited until Maxie had settled herself near the back of the room, then took a seat up front next to Palmer and Amy. Maxie's dad's show was just starting. Soon everybody, including Shanon, was giggling. Maxine Schloss's tall, redheaded father was hilarious! Everything about him, from his face to his baggy pants, was comical. Shanon, stealing a peek at Max to catch her reaction, was surprised to see that her roommate, unlike everyone else in the room, wasn't even smiling. In fact, as the room erupted into loud laugher, Shanon saw Max wince.

"Oh, my gosh!" howled Amy. "His pants fell off!"

Shanon found herself laughing even harder. Maximillian

Schloss was clearly about to lose his whole outfit! And beneath the clownish clothes he'd been wearing, he was dressed like a woman in tight jeans!

"Oh, no," Max groaned loudly. "He's doing that old 'Christina Jean Queen' routine!" She threw her hands over her face.

"Oh, wow!" Kate shrieked, "it's incredible! Now he's putting on roller skates! He's going to try to skate in those tight jeans!"

"He's the funniest-looking man—or should I say woman?—I've ever seen in my life!" Brenda announced above the laughter.

Shanon watched in sympathy as Max's face turned as bright red as her hair. It was obvious to her by now that Max did not think her father's "Christina Jean Queen" routine was nearly as funny as everyone else did. It had never occurred to Shanon that watching your own father play the clown in public might be a little bit embarrassing.

Shanon turned around and shot her roommate a look of sympathy, but Max's eyes were fixed on the floor. A moment later, she was on her feet.

"Hey, Max, where are you going?" Brenda asked.

"To my room for a minute," Max replied over her shoulder. Shanon couldn't see Max's face, but she heard a definite tremor in her voice. "I saw most of this show before in rehearsal," Max explained as she headed toward the door.

"Do you want us to tape it on the VCR for you?" Kate called after her.

"Sure, why not?" Max replied. "I'll watch the rest of it tomorrow."

Shanon followed her roommate out of the room and

found Max standing by the stairs. Her face was still red and her eyes were shut tight. Shanon reached out a hand to touch her.

Max's eyes flew open. "What do you want?" she demanded.

"N-nothing . . ." Shanon said. "I just wanted . . . You look bothered."

"I am bothered," Max said impatiently. Her brow was furrowed and there were tears in her eyes. Shanon stared at her for a long moment.

"Want to talk?" Shanon finally asked.

Max shook her head. She felt too embarrassed to speak. It was horrible hearing everyone laugh at her father. But how could she tell that to anyone, especially Shanon? Shanon's family seemed so *normal*. If Shanon, Amy, and Palmer had thought she was "unusual" before, she could just imagine what they must be thinking now. So without another word, Max turned her back and started upstairs.

As she watched Max go, a tear rolled down Shanon's cheek. She wasn't quite sure of all that was bothering Max, but one thing she knew for sure: The shoe was now on the other foot. Instead of being the one who disliked somebody, Shanon was the one who was disliked. And it didn't feel good.

CHAPTER 9

———◆———

"I hate to be a killjoy," Cora Davis said, "but it's past one o'clock in the morning. Even though it's a weekend, I think it's time you girls settled down."

"Okay, Mom," Shanon said. She and Amy and Palmer snuggled down in their sleeping bags. The Davises had created a cozy dorm-style room for Shanon and her friends in the basement.

"See you in the morning for pancakes," Shanon's mom said, clicking out the light.

"Good night, Mrs. Davis," Amy called out.

"Good night," Palmer echoed.

As soon as Shanon heard her mother go up, she clicked on the light again.

"Way to go!" Amy whispered with a giggle. "Let's stay up all night."

"I'm hungry," Palmer said mischievously. "How about raiding the refrigerator?"

"Good idea," Amy agreed. "That roast beef we had for dinner would make some good sandwiches."

"Shhh!" warned Shanon. The three girls listened. "No,

it's okay," she whispered. "I thought I heard my mom coming downstairs again for a minute."

"I don't hear anything," said Amy, sitting up on her elbows.

"Even so, we'd better wait awhile before we sneak up to the kitchen," Shanon said. "My mom's great, but she can be kind of strict."

"Okay," Amy said cheerfully. "What shall we do?"

"I know!" exclaimed Palmer. She jumped up, tiptoed across the room, and grabbed her overnight case. "Let's give each other manicures!"

"I don't need one," said Amy, looking at her neatly filed fingernails.

"Me neither," said Shanon. "Anyway, I've been biting my nails so much they're too short."

"Worried about something?" Amy asked.

Shanon shrugged. "We had that French quiz," she hedged. Actually, she'd been feeling bad about Max. It made her nervous living in a room with someone who hated her. But she didn't really want to talk about it now. This weekend she wanted to put Max completely out of her mind.

"Well, if we're not doing manicures, what *are* we going to do?" said Palmer.

"I know what," Amy said. She reached out for her guitar. "Let's practice the song for Shanon's grandmother."

"What's to practice?" Palmer objected. "All we're going to do is sing 'Happy Birthday.'"

" 'Happy Birthday' in *harmony*," Amy reminded her. She strummed the guitar softly. "Now, do you remember your note?"

"How could I forget?" Palmer said, rolling her eyes.

76

"I'm singing the melody. I don't need to practice that."

"Okay," Amy said, playing a chord. "Then I'll sing my new song."

"Shhh!" Shanon hissed. "You'll wake the whole house up."

"Sorry," Amy said, glancing toward the ceiling. "I forgot about that. I'll play you my song tomorrow. It's for John," she added with a big grin. "Kind of a follow-up to that rap song he wrote."

"I think John is really cute—for a dweeb," Palmer sighed, stretching out in her sleeping bag. "Of course, he's not the same type as Sam. Sam is more glamorous. But I think John really, really likes you."

"Thanks," Amy said. "I hope so."

"How do you feel about him?" asked Palmer with a gleam in her eye. "Do you really, really like John?"

Amy shrugged and smiled. "I think so. It's hard to say exactly how I feel."

"Don't you like him a lot?" Palmer persisted, sitting up on one elbow. "I like Sam a lot. I think about him all the time."

"I think about Mars, too," Shanon admitted.

"I guess I think about John," Amy confessed. Her dark eyes lit up. "I was writing about him in my journal the other day," she confided.

Palmer and Shanon giggled.

"What did you write?" Palmer asked eagerly. "Can we read it?"

"Gee," said Amy. "I don't know."

"I'll read what I wrote in my journal about Sam," Palmer volunteered, reaching for the thin canvas book in her overnight bag.

77

"Okay," Amy agreed. She looked at Shanon. "What about it? Do you want to read our journals to each other?"

"Gosh, I don't know," Shanon said with a blush. "The things I write are kind of private."

"What's so private about how we feel about our pen pals?" Palmer demanded. "We read all their letters to each other."

"Oh, it's not that. . . ." Shanon hesitated, recalling the mean things she'd written about Max. "I just write all kinds of other stuff that might be boring."

"Well, pick out the good parts," Amy suggested, smiling.

"Right," said Palmer. "We'll each read one juicy passage—that's all."

"And the person whose journal it is gets to pick it out?" Shanon asked.

"Sure," Amy said agreeably. Stretching out on the floor, she began leafing through her book. "I'll go first," she said. "You'll probably think this boring rather than juicy though."

Dear Diary,

Today I was thinking about John Adams and wondering if I wanted him for a boyfriend. I do think he's handsome, but I'm not sure he's my type, since he's so preppy. I definitely had something against preppies before I met John, but now I don't know. Maybe it's okay to be friends with someone whose style is different from yours, but I'm not sure a person should choose a boyfriend whose style is different. There is a boy who went out on a date with me in New York that I might like better. But if I went on a date with John in New York, I might like him better, too.

"Wow!" said Palmer. "You went out on a date in New York? Why didn't you tell us?"

"It was a group date," Amy explained. "To a concert. This boy was sitting next to me. He looked a lot like John, but his style of dressing was different."

"Are you going to invite John to New York?" Shanon asked.

"Maybe," said Amy. "I don't know. It's just something I wrote in my journal."

"This is fun," said Palmer. She tapped Shanon's leg with her foot. "Your turn. . . ."

Shanon blushed and moved over. Keeping her journal close to her chest, she searched for a mention of Mars. "Here's something," she said.

Dear Diary,

Sometimes I wonder whether it was fate that I met Mars Martinez and he became my pen pal. He is such an important person in my life. He loves animals, and so do I. He has such a great sense of humor and I love his dimples. When he holds my hand I feel a special feeling.

"That's so romantic," commented Amy.

"I know that special feeling," Palmer exclaimed. "I have it every time I see Sam. Even when I see one of his letters in my mailbox, I have it. First my heart gets this burning sensation. Then it starts turning over and over."

Amy guffawed. "Sounds like indigestion to me!"

"It doesn't *feel* like indigestion," snapped Palmer. "If

you don't recognize what I'm talking about, I guess you and John will never be boyfriend and girlfriend."

"If that's the way it feels, I'm not sure I'd want to," teased Amy. "We're not all the corny type."

"Corny?" Palmer sputtered.

"Quiet down," Shanon warned. She leaned over and gently tugged one of Palmer's curls. "Read yours."

"I thought you'd never ask," huffed Palmer, opening her book.

Dear Diary,

Every day I dream of Sam O'Leary. He's blond and has the most beautiful gray eyes. He is the drummer of my heartbeat, beating out the rhythm of my life. I hope with all my being I will see him again soon, playing with The Fantasy. Maybe I can get him to name a song after me.

Amy tittered. "A song named 'Palmer'?"

"Why not?" Palmer said nonchalantly. "Lots of songs are named for girls."

"It's a nice idea," Shanon said, trying to smother a giggle. "I wonder what Sam would think if he knew that he was the 'drummer' of your heart."

"That does it," Palmer said, slamming her book closed. "Here I thought up a fun activity for us, and all you can do is laugh at my most private thoughts. You did say that's what the journals were for when you gave them to us," she said, challenging Shanon. "Didn't you?"

"Of course," Shanon said. She gave Palmer an apologetic look. "Sorry I laughed at you. You were just so serious-looking when you were reading."

"I *am* serious," Palmer sighed, laying her head down. "I

think Sam is wonderful. I can't wait to see him at—" She sat up with a gasp. "Oh, my gosh, I completely forgot!"

"What did you forget?" Shanon asked. "Something about Sam?"

"Not exactly," Palmer groaned. "I invited Georgette to go to town with me this morning—I promised to introduce her to Sam. But when you asked us for the sleepover, I got so excited that I forgot."

"Too bad," Shanon commiserated. "I hope your sister wasn't too disappointed."

"Georgette will understand when you explain," Amy said reassuringly.

"I hope so," Palmer said. "We've been getting along so much better lately."

Shanon stretched out and yawned. "I wonder what time it is."

"I bet it's two o'clock in the morning," Amy whispered back.

"I'm hungry," said Palmer, getting up again. "Think it's safe for us to raid the refrigerator?"

"Why not?" Shanon said with a grin. "When else are we going to get a chance to stay up all night?"

"That's right," said Amy. "We've got to take advantage of this. After we eat, maybe we should all write letters to our pen pals."

"I'm getting punchy," Amy giggled as the girls tiptoed across the room.

"Me, too," Palmer admitted, "but I still want a roast beef sandwich, or maybe some of that apple pie would be better."

"Let's have apple pie!" Shanon whispered, testing the stairs. "Remember last year's sleepover?" she said, smoth-

81

ering a laugh. "Lisa ate the cinnamon rolls my mom was saving for breakfast."

"I remember," Amy said, giggling again.

Shanon sighed. "Too bad Lisa isn't here this year."

The girls crept silently into the upstairs kitchen. Then, while Amy and Palmer stood to one side, Shanon carefully opened the refrigerator and took out the pie. "We'll save the roast beef for lunch tomorrow," she said.

"Yum," Palmer whispered greedily. "I'm *glad* Lisa's not here! Apple pie is one of her favorites, and it's mine, too! If Lisa were here, she'd try to gobble it all up!"

Amy looked thoughtful. "I'm sorry Maxie couldn't come."

Shanon got out some plates, and the girls took seats. "Max was invited," she said, slicing the pie. "She could have come if she wanted to."

"Just like she could have a pen pal if she wanted one," Palmer added. "Max doesn't want to do anything with us lately."

"I did get her to say she'd try out for the basketball team," Amy said, digging into her dessert.

"That's not the same thing," countered Palmer. "Doing something on a team with you is not like doing something with the whole suite."

The girls ate in silence.

"It's all my fault," Shanon said finally. "Max hates me."

"I'm sure that isn't true," said Amy. "The two of you are just different."

"Yes, we *are*," Shanon said with emphasis. "And I'm afraid that we just don't like each other. I've tried and—"

"Maxie's tried, too!" said Amy protectively.

"Then why isn't she here tonight?" Shanon challenged.

82

"It's because the two of you hate each other," Palmer said with a yawn. "Let's drop the subject."

Amy's eyes drooped. "I guess we should. But we'll have to do something about it someday," she added. "If you live with a person, you've got to get along. It's not much fun for me and Palmer having Shanon and Max hate each other."

"But I don't hate her," Shanon protested. "She hates me!"

"Well, I think that Max thinks that *you* hate *her*," Amy pointed out. "So all you have to do is find a way to show her you don't. . . ."

"Max's birthday is coming up," Shanon said after a pause.

Amy blinked. "What? How do you know?"

"She told us on the first day of school—remember?" She sighed. Last year Lisa had given Shanon a surprise birthday party. But since she and Max were enemies, if Shanon gave Max a party, she'd probably hate it.

Shanon got up and put back the rest of the pie. When she turned around again, Palmer and Amy were both dozing.

"Come on, guys," Shanon whispered. "You can't fall asleep here. Let's go downstairs."

"I'm sleepier than I thought I was," Amy murmured, lifting up her head.

"I was going to write a letter to Sam," Palmer said, dragging herself to the stairs.

"You can do it tomorrow," Shanon said as she led her suitemates back down to the basement. In three seconds flat, Amy and Palmer were both fast asleep. Shanon picked up her notebook—she owed a letter to Mars and one to Lisa. She decided to write Lisa's first.

Dear Lisa,

Tonight we've been sleeping over at my house. We were trying to stay up all night like we did last year, but Amy and Palmer didn't make it. I don't know if my new roommate would have made it, because she didn't even come. She hates me. If you have any ideas on how two people who hate each other and have to live together can get along, please write.

Good night. I'm going to sleep.

Love,
Shanon

P.S. I miss you.
P.P.S. I'm glad you've got a new friend.

The next morning before breakfast Sharon wrote her letter to Mars:

Dear Mars,

How are you? How would you like to come to a book fair? Of course, in addition to all the books and tables, there might be some interesting people, too—like the Foxes of the Third Dimension! Seriously, I hope you can make it. I have been trying not to knock my new roommate, but things still haven't worked out. I'm not sure why. Hope to see you soon. Say hello to Ricardo! I'm at home this weekend for my grandmother's seventieth birthday. Today, I'm helping my mother bake the cake!

Love,
Shanon

Palmer and Amy also wrote to their pen pals:

Dear Sam,

I know you like to read, so guess what? I'm inviting you to the fall book fair at Alma. There will be refreshments! Please let me know right away if you're coming. Isn't it great that there's no rule against inviting Brighton students to Alma this year?

> Much love,
> Palmer

P.S. I think I am getting along a lot better with my step-sister. I was going to introduce you to her this weekend, but I just forgot.

Dear John,

Here is my answer to your ultra-cool and outrageous rap song.

> So you're back in school
> And you think you're cool
> Give me a break—
> You ace everything that you touch:
> Suede, metal, leather, steel in an automobile.
> Don't think you can give us the brush
> Yes, you're one of a kind
> But I won't flatter your mind—
> Welcome back, Jack! Welcome to school!

What do you think? It could be put to music. So if you come to the book fair, we can find a quiet corner somewhere and jam. Okay? We are having a nice weekend at Shanon's house. Maxie, the new girl in our suite, didn't come. Too bad—I think she would have had fun.

> Truly yours,
> Amy

CHAPTER 10

"It's the meanest thing I've ever seen in my life!" Amy wailed.

"Who could have done something like this?" Palmer moaned.

Shanon stared at the torn photograph on the sitting-room coffee table. It was the group picture she'd had blown up—the one with Lisa and all their pen pals! Before the three girls left for the weekend, it had been sitting on the bookcase. Now it was on the coffee table, ripped almost exactly in half!

"The person who did this meant for us to see it," Shanon said grimly.

"*Who* could have done it?" Amy exclaimed.

Palmer swallowed. "Maybe we have some enemies we don't know about, or maybe I . . ." Her voice trailed off and she looked away.

Suddenly Shanon turned to the door. "*I* know who did it," she said, "and I'm not going to let her get away with it!"

"Where are you going?" asked Amy.

"Hey, wait," called Palmer. "I think I know who—"

But Shanon was already out the door. There was only one person who could have destroyed the photograph, and that was Maxine Schloss! Max hated her—and Lisa! Not only that, Max had been the only one in the suite all weekend.

Shanon flew out of Fox Hall and tore across the quadrangle. She had to stop for a moment to catch her breath, and that's when she glimpsed a flash of red hair in the distance. It was Max, by herself, walking Gracie.

Shanon took off again, and moments later she was at Max's side.

"So, there you are!" Shanon blurted out. Ordinarily, she hated confronting people, but her feelings about Max had been building up for so long. And now her roommate had gone too far! "If you have something against me, you don't have to take it out on Amy and Palmer," Shanon continued, so angry she was hardly able to speak.

Max stopped and pulled Gracie's leash in. "I didn't know you were back," she said, looking bewildered.

"Yes, we just got back!" Shanon sputtered, folding her arms across her chest. "And we didn't like what we saw when we got here!"

"Did I leave the place a mess?" Max asked. "Sorry. I've been out with Gracie since morning." She stooped down to pet the dog. "I taught her to heel," she announced proudly.

"Stop changing the subject," Shanon cried. Tears of anger sprang to her eyes. "Ever since you moved into 3-D, you've had something against me. Admit it!"

Max tossed her head in anger. "It looks like you're the one who has something against me!"

"That's not true," said Shanon.

87

"It *is* true," said Max, "and there's nothing I can do about it. I'm sorry I took Lisa's place, okay? I'm sorry I'm not perfect like she is!"

"Lisa isn't perfect," Shanon said hotly, "but at least she wouldn't—"

"Don't change the subject!" Max yelled. "All you do is talk about Lisa! It's like a broken record!"

"She's my best friend," Shanon yelled back.

Max turned away. "Who cares?"

"I can't believe you did this!" Shanon cried, following along, nearly out of breath. "I can't believe you'd stoop to destroying personal property!"

Max frowned. *"What* are you talking about?"

"I'm talking about our pen-pal photograph you tore up!" Shanon said. "If you hate me, all you have to do is say it! You don't have to ruin something valuable like that and leave it for all of us to see."

Max's green eyes narrowed as she turned to face Shanon. *"I* didn't tear up any photo."

"Well then, who did?" Shanon demanded.

"I don't know," declared Max, "and I don't care. All you ever think about is Lisa, anyway! And your pen pal! You don't have time to even talk to anyone else."

"I talk to you," Shanon protested, rather lamely.

Max continued to stare at Shanon. She was holding Gracie's leash tightly in one hand. "You called me a klutz—" she said.

"I don't remember that," Shanon cut in. "Besides, you call yourself a klutz all the time."

"That's different," Max said, pulling away.

"What about you?" Shanon said accusingly. "You made fun of my favorite author! It just so happens that Elaine

88

Jones loves Michelle Wise! In fact, I suggested that we raffle off tickets at the book fair and that the winner would get to have lunch with *my* favorite author!" Shanon sputtered, hardly able to contain herself.

"Is that so?" Max shouted. "It just so happens that Mrs. Jones liked my idea, too! People are going to dress up at some of the book-fair tables! And even though *you* don't think it's *literature,* they're also going to sell science fiction!"

"Science fiction!" Shanon gasped. "I can't believe it!"

"Of course not!" Max cried in frustration. "That's because it was my idea! Anything I could ever think of, you'd think was silly! Anything I could ever think of, you'd hate!"

Gracie began to bark. Max and Shanon had been standing there yelling at each other in the middle of the quad. Both of them were feeling so hurt and angry they were almost in tears. Around the fringes of the yard, a few girls watched with curiosity.

"We'd better shut up," Shanon whispered in embarrassment. "People are staring."

"I don't care," Max replied, her voice shaking.

"However you feel," Shanon said, attempting to control herself, "it didn't give you the right to tear up our photograph."

"*I* didn't do it," Max repeated angrily as they walked past the gapers toward the dormitory. Shanon just shook her head in disbelief.

"I think we'd better see Maggie," Max said, once they were alone again.

Shanon rolled her eyes. "We're big girls now. I think we can handle our own fights."

"Maybe so," Max said bluntly, "but I need a new roommate."

Shanon followed Max into Fox Hall. Shaken by their argument, she was even more taken aback by this swift turn of events.

"It's obvious that we're terribly mismatched," Max said outside the faculty residents' door. "I may have to go to Alma Stephens, but I don't have to live in Suite 3-D." Max knocked and let go of Gracie's leash. The little terrier began to bark.

"There you are!" Maggie Grayson-Griffith cried, opening the door and bending down so Gracie could jump into her arms. "Thanks for giving her an extra walk today," she continued, smiling at Shanon and Max. "Dan and I were just saying the other evening that if we ever have kids . . . well, the best place in the world would be Fox Hall, with all you eager baby-sitters."

Shanon swallowed and looked down at the floor.

"We need to talk to you," Max said.

"Something private?" asked Maggie, ushering them inside.

"Not really," Max said. "It's just that we don't want to be roommates anymore."

Maggie glanced at Shanon. "Is that true?"

"I guess," Shanon muttered. "Yes, it's true," she said firmly. She'd never thought things would go this far, but if Max wanted to move, it was her decision. "We're too different."

"I'm not sure that's a good enough reason," Maggie advised.

"It isn't just that," Max volunteered. "We . . . we hate each other."

90

Maggie peered at the roommates. Shanon's face turned crimson and so did Max's.

"Those are very strong words," said the young teacher. Her violet eyes were sad. "Maybe if we talked things over together."

"It wouldn't do any good," Max said crisply. "We've made up our minds." She glanced at Shanon. "Haven't we?"

"Yes, we have," Shanon said, sounding determined.

"All right," Maggie agreed. "Who'll be moving out?"

"Not me," Shanon said in alarm. She glanced at Max. "Suite 3-D is my home here."

Max shrugged. "It makes no difference to me," she said. "I don't care where I go."

Maggie shook her head. "I'm sorry you feel that way, Maxine," she said. "You'll have to apply for a new room. And I'm afraid there isn't anything left in Fox Hall."

"That's okay," Max told her. "I'll leave the dorm if necessary."

Maggie turned back toward the apartment door. "It'll take a couple of weeks," she said. "There's always a waiting period in these cases and a certain amount of red tape." She looked hard at both girls. "Frankly, this kind of thing doesn't happen very often. Part of living together is learning to work things out. Of course, if your differences are irreconcilable—"

"They are," Max broke in.

"Okay," Maggie said. "I'll see what I can do."

"Thank you," Max said stiffly.

Shanon sighed. "Yes, thanks. . . ."

Shanon felt a strange churning in the pit of her stomach as the door closed behind them and Max walked off without a word. It had never occurred to Shanon that things would go this far. With a slow step, she returned to Suite 3-D.

"Did you find Maxie?" Amy asked.

"I found her," Shanon said without emotion. "She's moving out of the suite."

"She's doing what?" Amy demanded.

"Moving out," Shanon repeated. "She told Maggie she wanted a transfer." Shanon slumped down onto the loveseat. "It's probably the best thing that could happen," she murmured. "We don't want to live with someone who could do something mean like tearing up our photograph."

"Maxie didn't rip up our picture," Amy said hotly.

"Georgette did," Palmer announced from the desk.

Shanon shot up off the loveseat. "Georgette?" she choked.

Palmer held up the two pieces of the photograph, which she was just taping together. "Right after you went charging out of here to get Max, I went to find my sister," Palmer explained.

"Georgette admitted that she tore the picture," Amy continued. "She was mad because Palmer forgot about taking her to town on Saturday."

"So just like that—she tore our pen-pal photo in two?" Shanon asked, incredulous. "I can't believe it!"

"You were ready to believe it about Maxie!" Amy complained.

Palmer placed the carefully repaired photo back in its frame on the bookcase. "Georgette has a real temper," she said matter-of-factly. "She didn't really mean any harm."

"Oh, no," Shanon groaned. "What have I done?"

"Poor Maxie," Amy said. "She must have felt awful when you asked her to leave."

"Actually, it was *her* idea. She decided to leave herself," Shanon said. "I can't say I blame her. I never even gave her a chance to defend herself!"

"Gosh!" Palmer interrupted. "Look at this." Still at the desk, she was bent over a journal.

"Whose journal is that?" demanded Amy.

"It's Max's," Palmer confessed guiltily. "It was lying here on the desk. I thought it was mine at first, so I—"

"So you just happened to open it and read it!" cried Shanon. "When Max finds out about this, she's really going to hate us! She'll never forgive any of us for anything!"

"I didn't do it on purpose," Palmer protested. "I just opened it up and I saw something that . . . that I couldn't help reading!" She shut the journal quickly and pushed it away. "It was something she wrote about us," she added.

"About us?" Amy asked. "What was it?"

"It probably was about me," Shanon said grimly.

Palmer opened the book again. "Here," she said. "Listen to this:"

Entry in Max Schloss's journal—Saturday:
I can't believe how lonely I feel now that Shanon, Amy, and Palmer have gone away. I wish I hadn't turned down Shanon's invitation. I was so nervous about my dad's TV show that I almost bit Shanon's head off. Now she'll probably always hate me. It's so hard to be on the outside.

Shanon felt a pang. "Stop!" she said.

93

"Right. We shouldn't read any more," Amy added quietly.

Palmer shut the book. "Poor Max," she murmured. "Now she'll really think we're rats for reading her journal. Maybe we could read ours to her sometime," she said with a weak smile.

Shanon shook her head. "It's too late. She's moving out of the suite. Unless . . ." She slowly got up. "I'm scared to talk to her," she confessed.

"You have to," said Amy. "You have to apologize."

"I know," Shanon sighed. "But she's really mad at me. You should have heard us yelling at each other before."

"Georgette and I were yelling at each other, too," said Palmer. "But she said she was sorry."

"A little too late for that?" Amy suggested.

"Maybe not," Shanon said determinedly as she dashed out of the suite.

Shanon found Max on the other side of the quad. The tall redhead was standing under a tree in front of Booth Hall. Her eyes were red and swollen from crying.

"What do you want?" Max asked, quickly wiping her eyes with her sleeve.

"I . . . I don't know . . ." Shanon stammered. "To say I'm sorry, I guess. I just found out that you didn't tear up the photo."

Max stared at her. "Who did?"

"Palmer's sister," Shanon replied, hanging her head.

"I didn't even know what you were talking about," Max said. "I wasn't in 3-D all day. I was out with Gracie."

Shanon bit her lip as she remembered the words in Max's journal. "I should have let you explain," she said.

For a long moment both girls looked at the ground.

"Maybe having a fight was the best thing," said Max. "We've been getting on each other's nerves for a long time now."

Shanon was silent for a few seconds. "I felt kind of strange when Maggie said that most people work out their problems instead of getting new roommates. Maybe we could work ours out?"

"I don't think so," Max said.

Shanon hung her head. Instead of feeling glad to be rid of Max, she felt awful. "What about Gracie?" she asked. "Are we still going to walk her together?"

"Maybe we can take turns," said Max, "until I move out of Fox Hall." She looked back down at the ground and shuffled her feet. "What are you going to do now?" she asked, taking a quick look at Shanon.

Shanon sighed. "Go back to the dorm, I guess." She glanced around the quad. "That was some fight we had before. Good thing no one decided to call the police."

"Or Miss Pryn." Max grinned. "She would have had a fit."

"I've never been in such a big argument," Shanon confessed.

"Me either," said Max. "My brothers and I fight sometimes at home, but never anything like that." She almost chuckled. "They hate my trombone-playing."

"Really?" said Shanon. "I never even heard you play."

Max chortled. "Thank your lucky stars—now you won't have to."

The two girls walked slowly back to the dorm together. Shanon thought about telling Max how they'd read her journal but decided not to. Now that Max was moving out, there seemed little point in stirring things up.

95

"The trees are so pretty," said Shanon. "I like autumn."

"My favorite season is spring," Max muttered.

"Oh, my favorite is spring, too," Shanon added in haste. "But I still like autumn."

"So do I," Max admitted.

A melancholy feeling hung in the air as Max and Shanon entered Fox Hall and headed up to Suite 3-D.

"Maggie said it might be a while before you find a new roommate," Shanon said as she opened the door. "I guess we might as well try to get along . . . until it happens. I'm sure Amy and Palmer would appreciate it."

Max let out a sigh. "Okay. We'll have a truce."

"I wonder where Palmer and Amy are," Shanon said as they walked into the sitting room. "Maybe they're looking for us."

"Maybe they're already at dinner," Max suggested, collecting her journal from the desk and her books from the coffee table. She noticed the pen-pal photo on the bookshelf. "I see you patched the picture up."

"Palmer did," Shanon reported. "I really should have let you ex—"

Max shrugged. "I'm not mad about it anymore," she said. "It really doesn't matter because we won't be living with each other much longer anyway."

"That's right," said Shanon. She breathed a sigh of relief. "All of our problems are over."

Max began to whistle as they went into their room to change for dinner. "I look really weird," she exclaimed, catching a glimpse of her bloodshot eyes in the mirror.

"You're *not* weird-looking," said Shanon. "You should stop saying that. You're really very pretty."

Max made a clownish face. "I am?"

"I'm sure you already know that," Shanon said with a smile. "Anyway, I want you to know that if I did call you a klutz, I don't remember it and I'm sorry."

"I was listening at the door one day," Max confessed with a blush. "I heard you and Palmer and Amy saying things about me."

"Really?" said Shanon.

"You were talking about getting me a pen pal," Max continued quietly. "That's when I heard you say I was a klutz and Palmer said I was a giant and Amy said I was weird."

"We weren't really making fun of you then," Shanon said. "Honest, we weren't. And Amy didn't say you were weird—she said you were unusual. Being unusual is a good thing, and so is being tall. And I didn't really mean to hurt your feelings by calling you a klutz. I just said it because you say it about yourself all the time."

"The three of you really don't hate me, then?" Max asked.

"Of course we don't," said Shanon. "It was hard for me at first," she confessed, "losing Lisa—"

"Did you really want me to come to your house this weekend?" Max broke in.

"I really did," Shanon said with all sincerity. Her face flushed. "But I could tell you didn't want to come."

"But I did," Max said. "Only I thought . . ."

The two girls giggled.

"We really misunderstood each other," said Shanon. "It's so strange: what we *think* people are thinking about us may not be what they're *really* thinking."

"Come again," said Max quizzically.

Shanon laughed. "Sorry. Sometimes I'm too serious."

"Being serious is a good thing," Max protested.

"Thanks," Shanon said. "So is being funny."

"We'd better get going to dinner," Max said, jumping up.

"Sunday night is grilled cheese and bacon," Shanon said.

"Having that fight gave me an appetite," Max joked.

"Actually, I think it made me feel better," Shanon admitted.

Max sniffed. "It definitely cleared the air. Sorry," she said. "Corny joke."

Shanon chuckled. The two girls looked into each other's eyes. Then, as if a curtain were slowly lifting, they both began to smile.

CHAPTER 11

Palmer and Georgette huddled together on the library steps while a brisk wind whipped the trees. A few red and golden leaves swirled in the air and on the ground near their feet.

"I want you to tell Shanon and Amy that you tore the photograph," said Palmer.

"Do I have to?" Georgette whined.

"Remember our deal," warned Palmer. "If we're going to get along better, we have to try not to hurt each other's feelings—and not to sneak around doing mean things to each other."

"I said I wouldn't do it again." Georgette pouted. "Why do I have to do something embarrassing like apologize to your friends?"

"Because the picture was their property, too," Palmer insisted. "Anyway, they won't hold it against you. Amy and Shanon are nice."

Georgette tossed her head. "Not like me, I suppose."

"I didn't say that," said Palmer.

"But you were thinking it," said Georgette.

Palmer stood up and looked at the younger girl. "Listen,

99

I understand why you tore up the photo. It was my fault—I broke my promise to you. All I'm asking is that you don't do something like that again."

Georgette smiled. "Okay, I promise. That is, if you promise that you won't treat me like poison ivy anymore."

"It's a deal," said Palmer. She pulled one of her sister's curls playfully. *Georgette wasn't really all that bad,* she thought. In fact, she was kind of cute sometimes. And nobody could deny that she was brilliant.

"Well, that's over," Georgette said. "Wait until I tell Daddy."

Palmer's blue eyes narrowed. "Tell Daddy what?" she asked suspiciously.

"That we've reached a mutual acceptance and understanding of each other," Georgette replied.

"Come again?" said Palmer.

"That we like each other now, silly," the girl said, standing up.

"Whew!" said Palmer. "For a minute I thought you were going to tell him I was being mean to you."

"That would be stupid," said Georgette. "Then he would find out that I had been mean to you. You have to be very careful about what you tell Daddy," she said with a wink.

Palmer sighed. "Don't I know it!"

A cold gust of air blew across the steps, and Georgette pulled her cardigan closer. "Do I have to be careful what I tell *you?*" she asked Palmer seriously.

"What do you mean?" Palmer asked.

"Well, I'm the one who put that complaint about cliques in the *Ledger's* suggestion box," Georgette confessed. "Don't be mad, please," she begged, batting her eyes. "I was going to tell you . . . I'm sorry," she added, her voice faltering.

"Forget it," said Palmer. "How about some hot chocolate to celebrate our new understanding?"

"First of the season," said Georgette. "It'll be my treat." The two girls started walking toward The Tuck Shop. "How do you do it?" Palmer asked, recalling the conversation she and her sister had just had about their father. "Dad never gets mad at you. You really know how to handle him."

Georgette shrugged. "You just have to be clever."

"It's obvious that I'm not as clever as you are," Palmer muttered. "Dad is always on my case about everything— how much money I spend, my grades—"

"So what?" Georgette blurted out. "He still loves you more."

Palmer's face flushed. "He does not!" she said. "He definitely loves you more."

"You're his real daughter," Georgette said. "I'm not. Of course he loves you more than he loves me."

"You're his daughter, too," Palmer insisted. "He adopted you right after he married your mom, didn't he? He's always bragging about how smart you are. He thinks you're perfect," she exclaimed. "He definitely loves you more."

Georgette's face dimpled. "Wow, I hope so!" she said cheerily. As an afterthought she added, "I mean I hope he loves me as *much* as he loves you."

"Maybe we just shouldn't think about it," Palmer suggested. "Neither of us is living with him now anyway."

"That's right," Georgette agreed as they reached The Tuck Shop. "Now we're both living at Alma Stephens, and

101

we're each other's family." She dug into the pocket of her blazer. "Uh-oh," she murmured, rolling her big blue eyes.

"What is it?" Palmer asked.

"I'm afraid my funds have been depleted. I stopped by here earlier and—"

Palmer looked at her suspiciously and then smiled. "Okay, I'll pay for it—this time!"

While Palmer was having hot chocolate with her stepsister, Shanon was slowly making her way across campus toward the *Ledger* office. She'd just picked up her mail—a letter from Lisa that she couldn't wait to open—and was reading it as she walked:

Dear Shanon,

I'm sorry to say that things are not as great as they were when I last wrote to you. I thought my parents were getting along better, but Dad has still not moved back home. I had also thought that Betsy and I were going to be friends, and we are—but she has these other friends who belong to a club and they asked her to join it. They did not ask me. So now even though Betsy likes me, she spends most of her time with the girls in the club. So I'm feeling kind of lonely. I also have to admit that I feel jealous. Even though Betsy and I are different (she is into dating a lot, and as you know I am interested only in Rob!), we were having a lot of fun together.

Shanon, I am kind of worried about you. Your last letter sounded very strange. It's hard for me to believe that your new roommate could be so bad that you would hate *her. And how could anybody hate you? I ask myself. I remember that we had our share of fights last year when I was*

102

your roommate, however. Maybe you should give Maxine another chance. Maybe you can become friends like Betsy and I did. Since clubs are against the rules at Alma, you won't have the problem of feeling left out of things the way I do at the moment.

I hate snobs, don't you? It's so mean when people know you need friends and yet pay absolutely no attention to you when you're a newcomer. What can I say? I am different from a lot of people here—I've been away to boarding school and am just not part of their scene. I have the horrible feeling that they think of me as a snob. I even heard some people talking about me behind my back. What a bummer. I hate not being popular. I also hate what's happening with my parents. I also hate brussel sprouts and cauliflower, which my mother insists on feeding me. Plus I hate all the clothes they got me for school. At Alma we had to wear dresses or skirts and blouses to class, but here everybody wears sneakers and jeans. I was totally unprepared. I thought I had a neat wardrobe, but compared to the girls here who spend all their money on clothes I'm a total washout.

Please say hello to Amy and Palmer. Don't worry about telling people why I didn't come back. It's no big secret now, and it feels as if the whole world is getting separated or divorced anyway. And say hello to Maxine, or Max as you called her. You haven't told me too much about her except that you don't get along. Tell her that I think she is lucky to have you as a roommate. I hope you don't think this letter is sickening and that I'm feeling too sorry for myself. If you see Rob, please tell him that I miss him and I wish I were there. Also, try to remember exactly what he looked like and what he was wearing so that you can write

103

me every detail. (We're still writing to each other once or twice a week, but somehow it doesn't seem quite the same, knowing he's so far away.)

Love,
Lisa

"Of all the rotten things," Shanon muttered. Those stupid girls in Lisa's hometown! Didn't her friend have enough problems without people acting snobbish toward her? *People could be so mean,* Shanon thought.

Marching into the newspaper office, she slammed down her books. Kate wasn't around, so the office was quiet. The only sounds were the muffled cries of some girls playing soccer on the nearby field outside. Shanon clicked on her computer and started to write.

Leave It to Wanda

What Wanda wants to know is: Why can't people just accept one another for who they are? Whatever happened to the art of making a new friend? Some of Wanda's best friends happen to be people she thought she absolutely hated at first. But being a generous sort, Wanda decided to get past all that and find out who these people really were. Just because somebody dresses differently, or comes from a different place, or likes different subjects in school, doesn't mean that she might not make a good friend. Isn't variety the spice of life? Can you imagine going down the street and seeing that everyone you pass has the same face you do? Or has the same thing to say in exactly the same way? Or tells the same jokes or has the same sense of humor? Yuk!—that's what Wanda says.

According to my thesaurus, a clique is a "we-group" or

104

a "closed circle." But if there is a circle at Alma Stephens, it cannot include just a few. We have to have a circle, but it can't be closed—it has to have room in it for other people. So Wanda would like to join the staff of The Ledger *in welcoming all newcomers to our school.*

By the time Shanon finished her column, she wasn't thinking only of Lisa; she was thinking of herself, too, and of Max.

After storing what she had written in the computer, Shanon made a printout. Taking a seat at the desk again, she stared pensively at her first draft. A pale ray of afternoon sun fell across the paper. Things sometimes seemed so clear to her when she was writing them down—ideas that she could never say out loud. So she grabbed a pen and impulsively scrawled a note.

Dear Max,
Here is something I wrote today for The Ledger. *I wanted you to see it first. I'm sorry if I hurt your feelings. I am sorry that I didn't make my circle big enough.*

Yours truly,
Shanon

CHAPTER 12

"Did you get my note?" Shanon asked Max the next morning. The two girls were in the dining hall, having breakfast. She'd been waiting for her roommate to say something about the "Leave It to Wanda" column.

"I got it," Max replied, keeping her eyes fixed on her oatmeal.

Shanon took a sip of juice. "I wonder what's keeping Palmer and Amy?" she asked, turning her gaze toward their suitemates in the food line. "All they want is scrambled eggs."

"Maybe the chickens slept in," Max joked. "It *is* Saturday morning."

"I don't follow you," said Shanon after a moment.

Max shrugged. "You know . . . chickens . . . eggs . . . Saturday morning when people sleep late."

Shanon still looked bewildered.

"Oh, forget it," Max said, blushing. "I don't know why I'm always trying to make up jokes."

"Maybe because your dad is a comedian," Shanon suggested.

"That's probably it," Max agreed. She looked at Shanon wistfully. "Do you think my dad's funny?"

"Of course I do," Shanon replied. "Don't you?" she asked, remembering Max's strange reaction to her father's TV show.

"Sometimes I find it really embarrassing to watch him," Max admitted. "I know he's funny, but I guess since he's my dad . . ."

Shanon nodded in sympathy. "Sometimes I think my mom and dad are embarrassing, too."

Max smiled warmly. "Well, now that you've seen Christina Jean Queen, at least you know where my warped sense of humor comes from."

"You have a good sense of humor," Shanon said. "I was thinking that your idea about having a science-fiction table at the book fair with people dressed up like aliens might actually be kind of fun."

Max lifted her eyebrows in surprise. "Really? I was just thinking that your idea about making the book fair more serious was better."

"Well, we'll see how it turns out," Shanon said agreeably. "I heard that Mrs. Jones ordered a lot of different kinds of books this year, thanks to your suggestion. And I also heard that Michelle Wise is going to make an appearance."

"She's your favorite author," Max said with excitement. "That's great."

"I'm crossing my fingers that I win the raffle to have lunch with her," said Shanon.

"I read the rest of that book she wrote," Max said.

"Did you like it?" Shanon asked eagerly.

"It was kind of interesting," Max admitted. "I still like science fiction, though. You should try it sometime."

"Maybe I will," said Shanon just as Palmer and Amy finally joined them at the table.

"I think Mrs. Butter ran out of eggs," Palmer said, putting her tray down.

"Or else the chickens got run over crossing the road," Amy quipped.

Max giggled. "I guess I'm not the only one with a corny sense of humor."

"We'll have them in stitches on the basketball team," Amy replied.

"When do you find out if you made the team?" asked Palmer.

"The list goes up today," Amy said. "I'm going to stop by the gym after language lab."

"Speaking of languages," Max said, getting up, "I've got to write a paragraph describing a person, place, or animal for English class. I was thinking of describing Gracie."

Shanon giggled. "Did she heel like a good girl this morning—or did she nip at your socks?"

Max frowned. "I didn't walk her this morning. You did."

"No, I didn't," said Shanon in alarm.

"Uh-oh," Amy murmured. "Don't tell me you two forgot."

"We decided to take turns," Max explained. "I was sure that this was Shanon's morning."

"When I saw you go downstairs so early, I thought you'd gotten mixed up," Shanon explained, reddening.

"But it wasn't my day," Max protested.

"Let's go!" Shanon said, jumping up. "Maggie and Dan

said they had someplace to go early this morning. They were counting on us walking Gracie!"

"Oh, no!" Max gasped. "Their brand-new carpet!"

The two girls lit out of the dining hall, leaving Amy and Palmer behind. In no time they were back at Fox Hall. When they opened the door to the Grayson-Griffith apartment, Gracie came bounding up to them.

"No sign of damage," Shanon said, peering into the faculty residents' quarters.

"Let's get her out right away," Max said, grabbing the dog's leash.

In a matter of seconds, the girls were back on the quad with the growing puppy.

"Good girl, Gracie," Max cooed. "You were very patient this morning. Shanon and I almost forgot you."

"It was my fault," Shanon admitted. She glanced down at the puppy. "I think Gracie is so cute. My dog Sally is her mother. Did you know that?"

"Amy told me," Max replied. "I have a golden retriever at home. Her name is Honey."

"You do?" Shanon asked eagerly. "You never told me that!"

Max just shrugged. "I really miss her. Some people like cats, but I'm more of a dog person."

Shanon nodded. "I'm a dog person, too. Dogs are so loyal. They're always your friends."

"Yes, you can count on a dog," Max agreed. "Dogs are never mean on purpose, the way people sometimes are."

Shanon blushed. "You haven't said anything about my column," she blurted out.

"I think it's great writing."

"Really?" Shanon asked. "Thanks." They stopped to let

Gracie play with a flower. "What about the other part?" she continued. "The theme of it?" She felt embarrassed asking if Max had forgiven her, but she had to know.

Max's green eyes met Shanon's hazel ones. "I accept your apology," she said simply.

A lump rose in Shanon's throat. "Thanks." She took a deep breath. "I have something else to say. We read part of your journal."

The color drained from Max's face. "Why did you do that?"

"It was an accident," Shanon explained, red-faced. "Palmer thought it was *her* journal, and when she saw some stuff you'd written about how we'd hurt your feelings and you felt left out . . ." Her voice trailed off.

Max winced. "That was kind of private. I guess you thought I was a jerk, having my feelings hurt over practically nothing."

"I didn't think that at all," Shanon assured her. "I thought about what a crumb I'd been."

Responding to the jerk of Gracie's leash, Max turned away. "I think she wants to go for a run," she said.

"Let's do it!" agreed Shanon.

With Gracie in the lead, Shanon and Max dashed around the quad twice, laughing all the way. Then they tore back to Fox Hall. By the time they reached the dorm, they were all out of breath, including the puppy.

"Gracie's been such a good girl," Shanon said. "She definitely deserves a treat. Amy's got some dog yummies in her room. Let's give her some." And scooping the dog into her arms, she started upstairs.

"Hey, I thought it was against the rules to take her up," Max called after her.

"Nobody will care just this once," Shanon said recklessly. "Besides, the dorm is practically empty. Even Maggie and Dan aren't here."

Gracie seemed to love Suite 3-D! Darting into Palmer and Amy's room, she took a nosedive into the pile of clothes on the floor and headed out with one of Palmer's blue argyle socks.

"Stop her before she tears it!" Max yelled with a giggle.

Shanon wrested the sock away. The puppy made a flying leap for the pink loveseat. Max and Shanon laughed. Having fastened onto the pink slipcover, Gracie was tugging with all of her might.

Max balled up a piece of paper. "Here!" she called to the puppy. "Fetch!"

Turning instantly, Gracie leapt into the air, catching the paper ball in her mouth.

"Nice catch!" said Max. "She's going to make a good ballplayer."

"She's a great dog, all right," Shanon agreed, kneeling down to pat Gracie. "She was the pick of the litter, even though she is kind of rambunctious. At Maggie and Dan's wedding, she got out of her box and almost ruined the ceremony."

Max gasped. "You're kidding!"

"It was hysterical," Shanon said, laughing at the memory. "If it hadn't been for Lisa—" She stopped short.

"I don't mind if you talk about Lisa now," Max said cheerfully.

"Even though I've been 'a broken record'?" asked Shanon.

"It's fine to talk about Lisa sometimes," Max told her. "After all, she's your best friend."

Shanon sighed. "She's having a pretty hard time lately. Her parents are having marriage problems," she confided.

"What a bummer," Max said seriously. But then she burst out laughing as Gracie began yipping from under the desk. While the two girls had been talking, the feisty dog had tipped over the wastebasket.

Shanon couldn't help laughing, too. "Stop that, you naughty puppy," she said playfully. She crossed to the shelf beneath the window where Amy kept the dog biscuits. "If you don't behave like a good guest, you won't get your yum—" Shanon stopped abruptly. Something outside the window had caught her attention.

"What are you staring at?" Max asked.

Shanon turned around. "It's Miss Pryn," she gasped, lunging for Gracie. The puppy streaked away and disappeared under the loveseat. "We've got to get her out of here!" Shanon said frantically. "Suppose Miss Pryn comes up and finds her in our room!"

"Relax," Max said. "Just because Miss Pryn is outside Fox Hall doesn't mean she's coming up here." She peered out the window. "Who are those women with her, anyway?" she asked, observing the headmistress as she stood talking to a small group outside the entrance.

"Probably some visitors," Shanon said, her nervousness apparent. "Usually Miss Pryn doesn't do tours, but if the visitors are very special, she shows them around herself."

Max glanced out the window again. The stern-looking headmistress was on her way in. "Uh-oh," she moaned, "I guess Fox Hall *is* on the tour today."

"Oh, no," groaned Shanon. "I'll bet you anything she's going to come up here to 3-D!"

"Why would she do that?" asked Max.

"Because suites are unusual at Alma," Shanon insisted. "Most of the other dorms don't have them at all." Getting down on all fours, she reached under the loveseat. "Come out here this minute, Gracie!" she commanded.

"Maybe she's stuck," Max said, crouching down beside Shanon and peering under the small couch. "She's got another sock," Max reported. "Come on, pup," she beckoned, waving another dog biscuit. Gracie came out obediently and gobbled it up.

"Good girl," said Max.

Shanon breathed a sigh of relief. "Now all we've got to do is sneak her out of here."

Max picked the dog up. "I still think you're worrying about nothing," she said. "Just because Miss Pryn is showing some people around the dorm, that doesn't mean that she's going to come in here."

"Wait and see," warned Shanon.

At that moment, they heard the headmistress's voice and several pairs of high heels clicking up the stairs.

"They're coming to the third floor," Shanon whispered.

"What will she do to us?" Max asked.

"Not much I suppose," Shanon admitted. "Probably give us a demerit. It's what she might do to Gracie that I'm worried about. She might kick her out of the dorm altogether! She might not let Maggie and Dan keep her!"

"Oh, no," Max groaned, grabbing the dog. "That would be terrible!" She ran to the door. "I'll take her downstairs before they—" She opened the door, then quickly slammed it shut. Miss Pryn and her delegation were just a few doors away. "Too late," she whispered back.

"This is all my fault," Shanon said desperately. "When we gave Gracie to Maggie and Dan for their wedding, Miss

113

Pryn warned us. It's against some kind of code for us to have animals in our rooms. She gave Maggie and Dan strict orders to keep the dog downstairs."

There was a sharp knock on the sitting-room door.

"What are we going to do?" Shanon pleaded. "We have to hide her!"

"Hold them off!" Max ordered, ducking into her bedroom with Gracie in her arms.

No sooner did Max shut the bedroom door than the door to the sitting room creaked open. Miss Pryn and her group stood in the doorway.

"So there is someone here," the headmistress said crisply.

"Sorry, Miss Pryn," Shanon gulped. "I was just about to answer the door."

"Quite all right," the headmistress said. "We just want to look at the suite for a moment."

Shanon stood at attention, nervously eyeing the bedroom door. "It's kind of a mess today."

"Quite all right," Miss Pryn said, brushing by. She turned to the small group of women. "Suite living is quite new to Alma Stephens. In fact, it's still in the experimental stage. It provides a certain freedom and privacy for the girls, who have not only the common room downstairs to socialize in but their own very private sitting room right in the suite." The headmistress smiled at Shanon. "This is the second year in Suite 3-D for Miss Davis."

Shanon nodded politely and tore her eyes away from her bedroom door. She hoped Max had found a place to hide Gracie. Suddenly from behind the closed door she heard a shrill cry.

"What was that?" asked one of the women in the group.

"Sounds like a dog," said another.

Shanon shut her eyes. Gracie barked again.

"That *is* a dog," Miss Pryn said sternly. She marched toward the bedroom just as the door opened from the other side. Max stood in the doorway, coughing with all her might.

"Excuse me," she said between hacking.

"What a horrible cough," said Miss Pryn.

"Yes, I have an awful cold," Max choked. "I need some air!" Flabbergasted, Shanon watched her roommate lunge past the headmistress and dart quickly out the front door. Shanon noticed a pink—and wiggly—knapsack on her back.

"Tell Miss Schloss that she should check in at the infirmary," Miss Pryn said, tapping Shanon's shoulder.

"Yes, ma'am," Shanon said with a blush.

"Poor girl," said one of the visitors. "It sounds like the croup."

"Indeed," agreed one of the others. "A veritable barking."

As the group moved on down the hall, Shanon had to stifle a giggle. As soon as she could, she ran down the stairs to find Max. Her roommate was on the quad with Gracie.

"I can't believe you did that!" Shanon cried in amazement. "What nerve!"

"Did it work?" Max asked proudly. "Did they believe me?"

Shanon grinned. "One of them said you sounded like you had the croup! Then another one called your cough a 'veritable barking'!"

Max howled with laughter. "Like I said, I'm a dog person!" Shanon plopped down on the grass and laughed, too.

Max sat down next to her and Gracie curled up between them.

"Thanks for saving the day," Shanon said, grinning.

Max winked. "Any time. I wouldn't want Gracie to get expelled from school, even if I won't be walking her much longer."

"Why won't you be walking her?" Shanon asked in surprise.

"I'm moving out of Fox Hall," said Max. "Remember?"

Shanon lowered her eyes. "Gee, I'd almost forgotten."

"Hey, Shanon!" Amy's voice rang out over the lawn. She and Palmer were coming their way, waving envelopes. "We got some mail!"

Shanon jumped up with excitement. "From Lisa or Mars?" she asked as the two girls drew nearer.

Palmer slapped a letter into Shanon's hand. "From the famous Mars Martinez."

Shanon's eyes lit up. "Great. I hope he's coming to the fall book fair."

"Sam's coming," Palmer crooned. "I can't wait to see him."

"John is going to be here, too," Amy announced, showing Shanon an envelope. She turned to Maxie. "I stopped by the gym."

"Was the list up?" Max asked. "Who made the basketball team?"

"Neither of us," said Amy.

"Oh, no!" Max groaned. "Shot down again!"

116

"You win some, you lose some," Amy agreed. "I guess I'll go out for soccer, just like I did last year."

"Too bad you didn't make the basketball team," Shanon said, coming up to Max. She smiled at her sympathetically.

"No problem," Max said. "I'll find something else to join."

"So when are we going to read our letters to each other?" Palmer piped up. "Why not take them back to 3-D?"

"Fine with me," said Amy. "I can't wait to read you John's crazy new verse to the rap song."

Palmer and Amy turned toward Fox Hall. "Coming?" Shanon asked Max.

"I think I'll take Gracie home," Max said, picking the dog up. "Dan and Maggie will be back soon. They'll be worried."

"I'll come with you," said Shanon. "Then we can go upstairs to read our letters."

Max shuffled awkwardly. "I don't have any letters. I don't have a pen pal—remember?"

"That's okay," said Shanon. "You can listen to ours. Maybe then you'll change your mind about getting a pen pal of your own."

"What would be the point?" said Max. "I'm moving. Anyway, I don't think I'd know what to write a boy."

"We could help you at first," Shanon volunteered. "I was shy about writing to Mars last year. But then I got to know him through our letters."

"Hey, Shanon!" yelled Amy. "Hey, Maxie! Are you two coming or are you going to stay out here all day?"

"Hold your horses!" Shanon yelled back. "We're coming!"

Dear Shanon,
   I will definitely be there at the fall book fair.

                                        Luvya!
                                        Mars

Dear Amy,
   I was incredibly impressed with your verse to the song.
Yes, I'm coming to the book fair. The idea of finding a
place to jam together sounds delightful.

                                        Yours truly,
                                        John

Dear Palmer,
   A book fair sounds very interesting. Even more so be-
cause you will be there as well. I love to read, as you know.
I'll be on the lookout for you. I can hardly wait.

                                        Love,
                                        Sam

   Entry in Max Schloss's Journal—Saturday:
I think that Shanon finally likes me! And I think I like her,
too! I also didn't tell too many corny jokes today and
didn't spill anything. I did bark like a dog in front of the
head of the school, but it was for a good cause.
   I wonder who my new roommate will be. . . .

CHAPTER 13

"I can't believe that Michelle Wise came all the way to New Hampshire just for us," Shanon said, excitement in her voice.

She and Max were standing at the gym door on the morning of the book fair, selling last-minute raffle tickets. Max, dressed for work at the science-fiction table, was wearing a green spandex jumpsuit and a pair of towering antennae. Kate Majors came over to take the girls' picture.

"Great fair!" Kate enthused, clicking her camera. "Say 'Green cheese!' " she said, coaxing them for a smile.

Shanon and Max grinned and said "Green cheese" in chorus. Kate walked away chuckling. "We've never had such an exciting fair!"

On the other side of the gym Palmer stood with Georgette. "Truly innovative," said Georgette, glancing around. "Who thought of putting the cashiers in costume? The author's personal appearance is a good idea, too."

"Yes, it should be fun," Palmer agreed, keeping her eyes on the main door.

"Any sign of Sam?" Amy whispered, sidling up to Palmer.

Palmer shook her head. "Have you seen any of the other guys?"

Amy made a "thumbs-down" sign.

"What are you two whispering about?" Georgette asked, coming in closer.

"We're just waiting for our pen pals," Palmer explained.

"Oh, goody," said Georgette. "I'll finally get to meet Sam."

"I'll definitely introduce you," Palmer promised.

"Come and get me the minute he shows up," Georgette instructed. "I'll be over at the math and science table."

"What a dweeb," Palmer sighed, glancing after her stepsister.

Amy chuckled. "At least you two seem to be getting along better." She looked around the room. "This looks more like a circus than a book fair. Look at Maggie and Dan!" she said, pointing. Selling books at a table labeled "The Great Outdoors," the two teachers were dressed up like hikers.

"Cute," Palmer giggled. "That's probably what they wore on their honeymoon when they went camping in Nova Scotia." She glanced down at her own blue-flowered dress and matching blue pumps. "How do I look?" she asked.

"Very normal compared to everyone else," Amy said wryly. "But I'm sure Sam will think it's gorgeous." She nudged Palmer. "There he is, by the door!"

Palmer gulped. "Are you *sure* I look okay?"

"Great," said Amy, giving her a push. Watching Palmer greet her pen pal, she smoothed her own black leather skirt and fingered her necklace. Just behind Sam O'Leary, John Adams and Mars Martinez were arriving. Leaving Mars by the door with Shanon and Max, John headed straight for her.

"So *that's* the new girl in your suite, hey?" John said, glancing back at Max.

Amy giggled. "She's supposed to be an alien today." Blushing, she caught John's eyes. "Nice to see you."

The boy shuffled his feet. "Likewise," he said, flashing a smile. "Let's go check out the fair."

He grabbed her hand quickly, and Amy's heart did a flip.

"Sure thing," she said, trying to sound casual. "I saw something on the history of music over there. . . ."

While Amy and John browsed at the nonfiction table, Max took her post at the science-fiction table. Shanon led Mars to the popular literature books.

"How come this table is called popular literature?" Mars asked with a twinkle in his dark eyes. "Isn't all literature popular?"

Shanon giggled. "People have different tastes in things," she explained a bit self-consciously. "I suppose science fiction is probably considered popular literature, too. But we set it up in a different category, since my roommate likes it so much. We have the more serious novels, like Michelle Wise's, in this booth."

Mars laughed. "I guess those are the ones *you* like," he said. "Serious books for a serious girl."

"I hope I'm not *too* serious," countered Shanon.

As Mars reached for a book he touched one of her fingers. "Not too serious for me," he said, squeezing her hand. "I like serious things."

"How about this?" Shanon said with a blush. Trying to

act businesslike, she picked up a novel about baseball players. "I . . . I can tell you've gotten taller," she stammered.

"You're prettier," Mars blurted out.

Shanon gulped. "Want to check out the rest of the fair?"

Mars smiled. "Sure. I'll introduce you to my buddy Paul Grant. He's the blond guy over by the Outdoors table."

"Great," said Shanon. "Let's stop at science fiction and say hi to Max first."

In the middle of the gym, Palmer was introducing Sam to Georgette. They were having trouble hearing each other over the noise of the crowd.

"Nice to meet you," Sam said loudly, shaking Georgette's hand.

"Palmer has told me all about you," Georgette replied. "I really admire your ingenuity. It takes incredible talent and resourcefulness to write your own lyrics, perform in a band, and maintain yourself on the honor roll, the way you do."

"Coming from you, that's quite a compliment," Sam shouted.

"Well, I just wanted to introduce you to Sam like I promised," Palmer yelled, wishing Georgette would leave. It wasn't often that she got to see Sam, and she wanted some time alone with him.

"See you," Georgette cried, taking the hint. "I'm sure I'll run into the two of you later on." She tapped Palmer on the shoulder. "He has a lot of positive assets!" she said in a normal voice so only Palmer could hear.

Once Georgette was out of sight, Sam turned his full attention to Palmer. He put his arm on her shoulder as they walked to the refreshment table. "Your sister's sweet. You look kind of alike," he said. "Only you're much prettier," he added bashfully. He looked Palmer over. "*Nice* dress. It matches your eyes."

A blush crept up Palmer's neck. Sam's gray eyes were dreamier than ever! "Thanks," she said. "Everyone says that."

Sam chuckled. "Everyone says that your dress is the same color as your eyes?"

"No," Palmer said hastily. "Everyone says that Georgette and I look alike. Our personalities are very different, though."

"I'm glad," Sam said. "She's kind of verbose."

"That means talkative," Palmer said, nodding knowingly.

They smiled at each other. "Want me to buy you a cookie?" he asked. "Or better still, why don't we both go to The Tuck Shop for a soda?"

"What about the book fair?" asked Palmer. "I know how much you like to read."

"I can read at the Brighton library anytime I want," Sam said with a grin. "It's also kind of noisy in here. I'd rather go someplace where we can talk."

"Okay," Palmer agreed. "They're going to have the raffle drawing soon, but if either of us wins I'm sure Shanon will let us know. . . ."

Up front on the platform, Dan and Maggie Griffith had set up a microphone. An attractive brunette woman in her thirties was standing next to them.

"Okay, everybody!" Mr. Griffith's voice boomed across the gymnasium a little too loudly. The microphone let out a squeal and a few girls up front started to giggle. "I'll just adjust the mike a bit," the teacher muttered over the public address system.

"Way to go, Mr. Griffith-Grayson!" an anonymous voice called out.

"I heard that," Dan said good-naturedly. He stepped in closer and looked out at the audience, where Shanon, Amy, and Max were clustered near the back of the gym, listening. John, Mars, and their roommate Paul Grant were standing just behind them.

"First of all, let's have a hand for our librarian, Elaine Jones!" he said. There was a burst of applause as she stood up. "I think this is the most exciting fair we've ever had here! Many thanks to the Book Fair Committee!" The girls in the room clapped even louder. Mars gave Shanon a pat on the back. Then Shanon and Max smiled at each other proudly.

"And now I think I'll turn things over to my better half," Dan said, grinning at Maggie.

Maggie Grayson-Griffith took the microphone, and the girls applauded again. "I'd like to welcome you all to this wonderful book fair," the young French teacher said. "We have lots of special books here—and quite a few of them were written by one very special person. Say hello to our author from New York, Michelle Wise."

"She's beautiful." Amy raised her voice to be heard over the applause.

"She's really nice, too," Shanon said with admiration. "I already spoke to her."

Michelle Wise stepped up to the podium. "Alma Stephens is a wonderful school," the famous author began. "I wish I could sit down and have lunch with each one of you. But since this *is* a contest"—she flashed a friendly grin—"without further ado, I'll draw the winner!"

Excited murmurs filled the gym as the girls and boys inched up closer to the stage. Shanon crossed her fingers as Michelle Wise reached into a large jar stuffed with numbered tickets. Having lunch with her favorite author would be a dream come true!

"The winner is . . . number zero-three-two-five," the author announced, and there was a rustling of paper as the Alma girls and their guests checked their numbers.

Max gasped and held her ticket out to Shanon. "I think it's me!" she squealed.

"There's a name written on the ticket," Michelle Wise continued over the microphone. "Maxine Edith Schloss!"

Max threw her hands over her face. "Oh, my gosh! It *is* me!"

"Go ahead," Amy said, giving her a shove.

"Don't tell me you're bashful," teased Shanon.

"Max Schloss is back here! She's hiding!" John announced loudly.

All eyes turned to the back of the gymnasium. Max giggled nervously, then began making her way through the crowd. She couldn't believe this! It was the first time in her life that she'd ever won anything.

Amy nudged Shanon. "Disappointed?"

"A little," Shanon admitted. "But if somebody else had to win," she said with a smile, "I'm glad it was one of us!"

Shanon watched her roommate step toward the microphone. Max still had on her antennae.

"Is this the set of *Star Trek*?" the tall redhead inquired into the microphone. "I feel like an alien!"

The whole room started to chuckle, including Michelle Wise up front and Amy, Shanon, and their pen pals in the back.

Shanon beamed. Max had contributed a lot of good ideas to the book fair. And the drawing had been done fair and square. Shanon *was* truly glad her roommate had won. She also admired the way Maxie was handling all the attention. Up front on the stage, standing next to the author, Max seemed so poised, even with her antennae! And she looked terrific in her green spandex jumpsuit. Without understanding quite how it had happened, Shanon realized that she no longer disliked her roommate. In fact, she was beginning to really, really like her!

CHAPTER 14

—————◆—————

"Close your eyes!" Amy told Max.

"What for?" Max insisted. "Where are Shanon and Palmer?"

"Stop asking so many questions," Amy said, wagging her finger playfully. "It's a surprise."

Max closed her eyes and smiled. It was a Tuesday afternoon after gym class. It was also her fourteenth birthday. Though she didn't remember telling Amy, Palmer, and Shanon about it, she guessed that Amy had somehow found out. The last few days had been so neat. First there had been the book fair and then her lunch with Michelle Wise at a fancy restaurant in Brighton. But the best times of all had been right here in Suite 3-D. She and Shanon hadn't had a single argument!

The chords to Amy's guitar strummed a rollicking "Happy Birthday."

"You can open your eyes now!" Amy sang out.

Maxie's green eyes flew wide open. Shanon and Palmer were standing in the doorway, holding a chocolate cake ablaze with candles.

"You guys are too much!" Max exclaimed. A wide grin

lit up her face. "How did you know it was my birthday?"

"You told us the first day you arrived," Shanon said with a giggle.

"I did?" Maxie said, blushing. "Sometimes I talk so much, I hardly know what I'm saying."

Palmer put the cake in front of her. "Stop talking now and blow out the candles," she said with a twinkle in her eye.

Max took a deep breath, shut her eyes tight, and made a wish. Then she blew with all her might.

"Be careful," Amy warned. "You'll blow the icing off!" The four girls laughed companionably. Then Amy struck up "Happy Birthday" again, and she, Shanon, and Palmer sang the song in harmony. Max's eyes glistened with pleasure.

"Aw, shucks," she said, clowning around, "you all are making me bashful."

"*You* bashful?" Palmer said wryly. "That'll be the day!"

"You're right," Max replied. "Let's cut this baby up!" Grabbing the knife Shanon had brought along, she sliced into the cake and passed out huge servings to her suitemates.

"Yummy," moaned Palmer, licking some icing. "German chocolate cake is my absolute favorite."

"Shanon made it in the dorm kitchen," Amy informed Max.

"Delicious," Max said after taking a big bite. She gave Shanon an appreciative look. "Thanks a lot."

"I was glad to do it," said Shanon. "It's your birthday— and you still are my roommate."

There was a knock on the door and Maggie poked her head in.

"Hi, Ms. Grayson-Griffith!" Max sang out.

"Happy birthday," Maggie greeted her. "Dan and I want you to come down to the apartment later. Gracie has a little gift for you."

"Thanks," Max said with a grin. "I'll bring some of this yummy cake that Shanon made for me."

Miss Grayson-Griffith looked around the sitting room. "You girls have done wonders with this room. It's so cozy."

"Thanks," said Amy. "The wall hanging over the loveseat is Max's."

Maggie smiled. "It's lovely. . . ." She turned her gaze to Max. "I thought you'd like to know that your transfer has been approved," she said. "You can move over to Cabot Hall at the end of the week. A fourth-former named Lucy Gibson will be your new roommate."

"Oh, I know her," Palmer piped up. "She's got great clothes."

"She was on the hockey team last year," Amy added.

Max swallowed slowly. "Thanks," she said, lowering her eyes.

"I was glad to arrange it," Maggie said, turning away. "If that's what you girls wanted."

Shanon and Max glanced at each other, then looked away.

"Thanks for going to the trouble for us, Ms. Grayson-Griffith," Shanon said politely.

"No problem," Maggie said, heading out the door. She turned to smile at Max again. "See you downstairs after supper."

When Maggie left, the room grew quiet. All four of the girls looked down at their plates.

"Great cake," Max muttered, breaking the silence. She forced a wistful smile. "I think I'll offer some to Brenda and Kate and the other girls." She got up and brushed some crumbs off her jeans.

"Wait!" Shanon said, glancing over at Amy and Palmer. "I don't know how the two of you feel, but I've got something on my mind."

"Let's hear it," Amy urged with a hopeful look in her eye.

Shanon stood up to face Max. "I know you said that your mind is made up, but . . . I was wondering . . ." In a shaky voice, she went on: "I know I wasn't very nice in the beginning—"

"And I sneaked and read your journal," Palmer blurted out.

"But *I* was the worst!" Shanon cut in.

"I was pretty bad, too," Max said hastily. "All those corny jokes I kept telling, and I know I'm a klutz—"

"You're not a klutz," Shanon interrupted.

"I don't think so either," Amy said. She looked first at Shanon and then back at Max. "Won't you two say *something* to each other?" she prodded.

Max and Shanon burst into nervous giggles. Shanon slowly held out her hand. "What I have to say, Max, is that I don't want you to leave."

"Me neither!" Amy said firmly. "Suite 3-D wouldn't be the same without you."

"I agree," Palmer chimed in. "After all, you've already lived here for almost a month. We're used to you."

"Not only that," Shanon added, "but we like you."

Max took Shanon's outstretched hand and shook it. Her eyes flooded with happy tears. "I like you, too," she said, "and I really don't want to leave." She laughed and took a swipe at her eyes with her shirtsleeve. "What a dope," she mumbled. "I'm crying."

"I'm almost crying, too," Shanon admitted, sniffling and giggling at the same time.

"Well, *I'm* not crying," said Palmer. "I'm glad. Now maybe there will be some peace and quiet in this place. Things can get back to normal for a change."

Amy rolled her eyes. "*Normal!* Why does everything have to be normal?"

Palmer shrugged. "I just like it that way. Now it'll be just like it was last year. We'll really be the Foxes of the Third Dimension! And if Max is going to be one of us, she'll have to get a pen pal."

"Maybe Max isn't interested in that," Shanon said protectively.

"Well, maybe I *am* interested," Max replied.

"Outstanding!" cried Amy. "What changed your mind? I bet it was John's funny rap song!"

"No, it was probably seeing how cute Sam is," Palmer gushed.

"Why *did* you change your mind?" Shanon asked.

"I'm not sure," Max said, sticking her hands in her pockets. "Maybe I think it'll be interesting, that's all. Maybe it'll be an adventure to get to know someone through letters. Mars, John, and Sam all seem to be pretty nice guys."

"Let's put another ad in the Ardsley *Lion* right away!" Amy exclaimed.

"What should we say?" Palmer asked, grabbing a notebook.

Shanon settled back and munched some more cake.

"First of all, we'll have to say that Max is a very unusual person," she declared, her voice full of humor. "That she's very tall, has red hair, and is gorgeous."

Max rolled her eyes. "And that I spill things and will probably step on people's feet."

Palmer arched an eyebrow. "I think we can leave that part out. We want you to get a really good pen pal, just like we did."

"Someone who's intelligent," Amy offered, thinking of John.

"And humorous," Shanon said, thinking of Mars.

"I would say a rock musician," Palmer chimed in, "but I think Sam might be the only one of those available."

"Well, whoever it turns out to be," Max said excitedly, "I'm sure he'll be interesting!"

Palmer held up her notebook. "Listen to this," she said. "WANTED: BOY PEN PAL. PLEASE CONTACT MAX SCHLOSS, SUITE 3-D, FOX HALL, ALMA STEPHENS SCHOOL FOR GIRLS."

"Perfect," said Shanon. "Short and sweet."

"Just a minute," Max said thoughtfully. "So there's no mistake." She took the notebook and pen and added a line: P.S. I'M A GIRL!

Amy, Shanon, Palmer, and Maxie looked at each other with satisfied grins. For a moment Shanon felt a pang. Lisa would have really enjoyed this! But Shanon was also pretty sure that her old roommate would have liked Max, too.

"I hereby dub you an official Fox of the Third Dimension!" Shanon said, tapping Max on the shoulder with a pillow.

Palmer giggled. "How does it feel?"

"Feels great," Max said happily.

132

Palmer picked up her slice of cake. "To Max!" she cried.

"To Maxie," said Amy.

"To Max," Shanon said, smiling.

Max pointed to the photograph on the shelf. "Let's not forget Lisa! To the first Fox!"

Shanon gave Max a hug. Everything was going to be all right!

After putting aside two slices for Maggie and Dan, the four Foxes passed out birthday cake to the rest of their friends. The cake had looked rather small, but there was enough for everyone on the third floor!

Dear Lisa,

I got your last letter. I hope things are going better for you in school and that you and Betsy are spending more time together. I can't imagine you being lonely. At Alma you were so popular. I'm sure that the girls in your new school will soon find out what a great person you are. Things are much better here in Suite 3-D. Maxie and I are no longer enemies. In fact, we're friends! I think you would like her, too: She is funny and a real brain when it comes to science. I also found out that she actually does like flowers. When we went to Brighton last weekend, she got a huge bunch of daisies for the suite. When I asked her about it, she said she loves flowers—it's just that she hates flowered bedspreads. I'm also happy to say that she is not stuck up the way I thought she would be at first . . . you know, because her father is a famous person. It just shows you how people can be wrong about each other.

Please keep writing. We had the book fair again this year

and a lot of Ardies showed up. Sorry to say, none of us saw Rob. I'm sure he misses you just as much as we do.

Love,
Shanon

P.S. Amy, Palmer, and Max just came in and want to add something:
Hang in there, Lisa!—Love, Amy
Write me about the boys at Chestnut High!
Luvya!—Palmer
Hope to meet you someday! Love, Maxie!

Entry in Max Schloss's Journal—Monday:
Things couldn't be better at Alma Stephens these days. Shanon and I are really getting along. Now what's on my mind is my new pen pal! I'm kind of nervous. Yikes! I wonder who he'll be!

Something to write home about . . .
                              another new Pen Pals story!

Pen Pals #14

In Book Fourteen, THE MYSTERY ABOUT MAXIE, Maxie Schloss, the newest member of Suite 3-D, has to get with it. If she's going to be a Fox, she has to have a pen pal. Shanon, Palmer, and Amy convince her to place an ad in the Ardsley *Lion*. And what a terrific response! Now Maxie can't decide on a pen pal. Then a mysterious letter is delivered to Suite 3-D addressed to Maxie. Who is the mystery pen pal? What is he hiding?

P.S. Have you missed any Pen Pals? Catch up now!
        PEN PALS #1: BOYS WANTED!

Suitemates Lisa, Shanon, Amy, and Palmer love the Alma Stephens School for Girls. There's only one problem—no boys! So the girls put an ad in the newspaper of the nearby Ardsley Academy for Boys asking for male pen pals.

PEN PALS #2: TOO CUTE FOR WORDS

Palmer, the rich girl from Florida, has never been one for playing by the rules. So when she wants Amy's pen pal, Simmie, instead of her own, she simply takes him.

PEN PALS #3: P.S. FORGET IT!

Palmer is out to prove that her pen pal is the best—and her suitemate Lisa's is a jerk. When Lisa receives strange letters and a mysterious prank gift, it looks as if Palmer may be right. But does she have to be so smug about it?

PEN PALS #4: NO CREEPS NEED APPLY

Palmer takes up tennis so she can play in the Alma–Ardsley tennis tournament with her pen pal, Simmie Randolph III. But when Palmer finds herself playing *against*—not *with*— her super-competitive pen pal, she realizes that winning the game could mean losing *him*!

PEN PALS #5: SAM THE SHAM

Palmer has a new pen pal. His name is Sam O'Leary, and he seems absolutely perfect! Palmer is walking on air. She can't think or talk about anything but Sam—even when she's supposed to be tutoring Gabby, a third-grader from town. Palmer thinks it's a drag, until she realizes just how much she means to little Gabby. And just in time, too—she needs something to distract her from her own problems when it appears that there *is* no Sam O'Leary at Ardsley.

PEN PALS #6: AMY'S SONG

The Alma Stephens School is buzzing with excitement—the girls are going to London! Amy is most excited of all. She and her pen pal John have written a song together, and one of the Ardsley boys has arranged for her to sing it in a London club. Amy and her suitemates plot and scheme to get out from under the watchful eye of their chaperone, but it's harder than they thought it would be. It looks as if Amy will never get her big break!

PEN PALS #7: HANDLE WITH CARE

Shanon is tired of standing in Lisa's shadow. She wants to be thought of as her own person. So she decides to run for Student Council representative—against Lisa!

PEN PALS #8: SEALED WITH A KISS

When the Ardsley and Alma drama departments join forces to produce a rock musical, Lisa and Amy audition just for fun. Lisa lands a place in the chorus, but Amy gets a leading role. Lisa can't help feeling a little jealous, especially when her pen pal Rob also gets a leading role—opposite Amy.

PEN PALS #9: STOLEN PEN PALS

Shanon, Lisa, Amy, and Palmer have been very happy with their pen pals—but now they have competition! Four very preppy—and very pretty—girls from Brier Hall have advertised for Ardsley pen pals. And pen pals they get—including Rob, Mars, and John!

PEN PALS #10: PALMER AT YOUR SERVICE

Palmer's broke! Because of her low grades her parents have cut her allowance. Now she needs to find ways to make money and fast! The Foxes put their heads together to help Palmer with quick money-making schemes *and* to help her with her grades. But they can't do it all. Palmer has to help herself. But will snobby Palmer be able to handle a waitress job?

PEN PALS # 11: ROOMMATE TROUBLE

Lisa rearranges the suite so that all four girls sleep together in the sitting room. And when shy Muffin Talbot complains that Lorraine Murphy, her new roommate, is a monster, Lisa invites her to sleep in the suite, too. Soon Suite 3-D is so crowded Shanon can hardly study, so she studies in Lorraine's room—and starts to like Lorraine. But her suitemates, especially Lisa, think Lorraine is taking advantage of Shanon.

PEN PALS #12: LISA'S SECRET

What's wrong with Lisa? Not even Shanon can find out what's made Lisa change into a grouch overnight. She's irritable, moody, and snaps at everyone. She isn't even cheered up by an invitation to Maggie and Dan's wedding!

WANTED: BOYS — AND GIRLS —
WHO CAN WRITE !

Join the Pen Pals Exchange and get a pen pal of your own!
Fill out the form below.
Send it with a self-addressed stamped envelope to:

PEN PALS EXCHANGE
c/o The Trumpet Club
PO Box 632
Holmes, PA 19043
U.S.A.

In a couple of weeks you'll receive the name and address
of someone who wants to be your pen pal.

Cut here ---

PEN PALS EXCHANGE

NAME _____ GRADE _____

ADDRESS _____

TOWN _____ STATE _____ ZIP _____

DON'T FORGET TO INCLUDE A STAMPED ENVELOPE
WITH YOUR NAME AND ADDRESS ON IT!

Please check one
☐ I bought my book in a store.
☐ I bought my book through the Trumpet Book Club.